C A N D L E L I G H T
Ecstasy Supreme

"FEELING THREATENED?" DAMIEN RASPED.

"I'm terrified," Trish answered honestly. "It took me years to get over you. I could never go through that again."

"Hmm. I'm not sure I like hearing myself described as something that has to be gotten over. Nor do I like hearing that you were successful. But there's really no sense in arguing the point, is there?" He turned so that he was on his side and could see her face. "We both know you're lying."

"You still go for the throat, don't you?" Trish frowned.

"Where you are concerned, yes," he said bluntly. "I want you back. There's no other way of putting it." His hand on her waist tightened. "I want to be married to you again—I want you to have my baby. I want the same things I wanted five years ago."

CANDLELIGHT ECSTASY SUPREMES

HIDDEN MANEUVERS

Eleanor Woods

A CANDLELIGHT ECSTASY SUPREME

Published by
Dell Publishing Co., Inc.
1 Dag Hammarskjold Plaza
New York, New York 10017

Dell ® TM 681510, Dell Publishing Co., Inc.

Candlelight Ecstasy Supreme is a trademark
of Dell Publishing Co., Inc.

Candlelight Ecstasy Romance®, 1,203,540, is a registered
trademark of Dell Publishing Co., Inc.

ISBN: 0-440-13595-8

Printed in the United States of America
First printing—January 1985

To Our Readers:

Candlelight Ecstasy is delighted to announce the start of a brand-new series—Ecstasy Supremes! Now you can enjoy a romance series unlike all the others—longer and more exciting, filled with more passion, adventure, and intrigue—the stories you've been waiting for.

In months to come we look forward to presenting books by many of your favorite authors and the very finest work from new authors of romantic fiction as well. As always, we are striving to present the unique, absorbing love stories that you enjoy most—the very best love has to offer.

Breathtaking and unforgettable, Ecstasy Supremes will follow in the great romantic tradition you've come to expect *only* from Candlelight Ecstasy.

Your suggestions and comments are always welcome. Please let us hear from you.

Sincerely,

The Editors
Candlelight Romances
1 Dag Hammarskjold Plaza
New York, New York 10017

CHAPTER ONE

There was an air of impatience emanating from the tall, dark man as he alternated between pacing around the room and sitting for brief moments in the large leather chair behind the massive desk.

Waiting annoyed him; patience was not one of his virtues.

A heavy sigh of irritation hissed past Damien St. Clair's lips as he pushed back the cuff of his dark blue shirt and glanced at the heavy gold watch on his wrist.

Where the hell was Hal? He'd said eleven o'clock. It was now twenty minutes past.

Long, square-tipped fingers drummed against the cluttered surface of the desk. Hearing from Hal Langdon had been something of a surprise. Nice, but a surprise nevertheless. They'd roomed together at Harvard, served their time together with Uncle Sam, then gone their separate ways. Hal had chosen to remain with the government while

Damien returned to Texas to resume command of the vast land holdings that made up the St. Clair empire.

Damien had given his time to his country as he'd been taught was his duty. But making a career of anything other than ranching had been, and still was, alien to his way of thinking. He was a dyed-in-the-wool Texan. He'd cut his teeth on dust and cattle and—God willing—he'd die that way. The years he'd been away had merely increased his love for the land that generations of his family had fought and died for.

Suddenly the buzzer on the intercom sounded. Without shifting positions Damien reached over and depressed a button. "Yes, Margie?"

"Mr. Langdon is here to see you, Damien."

"Send him in."

The door opened, and the two men stared at each other, their expressions varying as thoughts of other places and times flooded their minds. Damien rose to his feet and stepped around the desk smiling, his hand outstretched. "It's been a long time, Hal."

"Too long," Hal answered, his homely face breaking into an easy grin as he let the door swing closed behind him. Then he walked forward and caught Damien's hand in his own. "How's the world treating you?"

"I'm managing," Damien said, chuckling.

"I'm managing." He eyed the considerable amount of blond hair missing from his friend's head. "And from what I can see, it looks as though I'm doing a damn sight better than you. What's happened to your hair?"

"Hazards of the trade," Hal said with a devilish gleam in his laughing eyes. "What's your excuse for that ugly puss I'm forced to look at? Don't you know any decent plastic surgeons?"

"Definitely not." Damien laughed, passing one large hand over his square chin and then his nose, which looked as though it had been broken in several places. There was also a tiny, narrow scar that ran from his right temple and disappeared into the coal-black thickness of his hair.

It was an interesting face, one that showed strength and force, but never one that could be called handsome. Dark blue eyes, framed by thick, sooty lashes, were the only softness nature had seen fit to grant.

"Sit down." Damien waved his friend to one of two leather chairs in front of the desk. "How about a Scotch and water?"

"Sounds perfect," said Hal, his gaze running curiously around the office. "When did you move in here? I didn't think anything could ever pry you loose from that ranch."

"Progress, expansion," Damien remarked dryly. He turned from the wall cabinet that held an assortment of liquor and glasses. "It's not like it used to be." He walked back across the room, handed Hal his drink, then sat down in the other chair. "It's confining as hell, but I manage to get away from time to time."

"You being stuck in an office is hard to believe," Hal said, grinning. "But then, you'd make any sacrifice for that ranch, wouldn't you?"

Damien shrugged one broad shoulder. "Almost." He raised his glass in a toast. "To the good times."

"To the good times," Hal echoed. He tipped the glass to his lips and then grimaced as the liquor slipped down his throat. "Damn! You're making them kind of strong these days, aren't you?"

"That's a strange remark coming from you." Damien chuckled. "I've seen the time when you could outdrink everyone in a bar, including me."

"That was in my carefree youth," Hal said resignedly. "These days, I'm afraid life is a bit more serious."

"Responsibility that heavy?"

"At times it is. And in my job you don't stay alive without all your wits about you."

"Well, maybe a few days at the ranch will give you a chance to unwind. It's probably been years since you were on a horse."

"It has," Hal said, "and I'd just as soon it be

12

a few more. I have a definite dislike for the animals. But I'm afraid I won't be staying over for a visit this time."

"Oh?" Damien asked curiously. "Are you here on business?"

"In a manner of speaking," Hal hedged. He made a circular motion with the glass he was holding, his eyes following the melting cubes of ice as the liquid swirled around inside. "I need your help—or, rather, there's another person who needs your help."

"All you have to do is ask."

"Don't be so hasty, my friend," Hal warned, his carefree expression replaced by a deadly serious one. "You might not be so generous when you know the identity of this person."

"Oh?" Damien countered. "Then suppose you stop being so mysterious and tell me."

"It's Trish. The problem is her possible involvement in drugs, and the fact that her life could be in danger."

Damien stared incredulously at Hal, his tanned face turning slightly pale as the words sank in. With motions reflecting the shock waves hitting his senses, he carefully set the glass on the edge of the desk, then dropped back against the chair. "Are you sure she's involved?" he asked in a hoarse voice.

"That is part of the mystery. If she does know something or is involved, then we have to find out—and quickly. I don't need to tell you what kind of people are involved in the distribution of drugs," Hal said quietly.

"Damn!" Damien exploded. He came to his feet in one powerful surge, his tall, lean body taut with tension. "You'd better tell me all of it."

Hal turned in his chair and watched his friend pacing around the room. For a man who had been divorced for three years and was supposed to have gotten over the breakup, Damien was certainly acting strange. That grimness reflected in his face wasn't the look of a man who had stopped caring for a woman.

"Are you sure you want to get involved in this, Damien?"

"Don't you think it's a little late to be asking that, Hal?" Damien swung around and faced him. "Weren't you pretty certain that the moment you mentioned my ex-wife's name I'd react just as I did?"

Hal shrugged, a sheepish look on his face. "Okay. I was counting on you offering to help. But I wasn't aware that you still cared—"

"I'm not interested in hearing your opinion regarding what you 'think' I feel, Hal. So why don't we deep-six all the psychological crap and get down to business."

"Are you aware that John Sanders was killed approximately three months ago?" Hal asked.

14

"John? Dead?" Damien asked in a stunned voice. He ran a hand around to cup his neck, a look of disbelief on his face. "How?"

"According to the coroner's report, his death was the result of a gunshot wound to the right temple. It was also suggested that he was shot by a burglar, who was surprised during an attempted robbery of the kennel," said Hal. "His death occurred shortly after his return from the dog shows in Mexico. On the trip back home he was involved in an automobile accident that left him with nothing more serious than a broken arm. One of his assistants wasn't so lucky, though. That young man was killed."

"How does all this fit in with Trish being involved in drugs?" Damien asked in a steely voice. Damn! he was privately thinking. How the hell could she do such a stupid thing? If she'd needed money why hadn't she called him? And why hadn't she let him know about John? Had she gotten involved with some man and been lured into this situation without really knowing what she was doing?

"According to reports from our agents in that area, it looks as though the island where Trish and her father lived was a distribution point of sorts for some rather hefty drug dealings. Evidence points to there being large shipments of cocaine, which just happened to coincide with each time John Sanders returned from one of his trips to the numerous dog shows he frequented."

"My God!" Damien paled, his body as controlled as a tightly coiled spring. "And Trish? Has she taken up where John left off?"

"That's what we don't know," Hal said honestly. "And just to set the record straight, Damien, we aren't sure John Sanders was involved willingly. He could have been blackmailed into it. We don't know to what extent, if any, that Trish is involved. What we are certain of is, as I said, large shipments of drugs, mainly cocaine, coinciding with the elder Sanders's trips. When he died, there was a sudden halt in the operations. Trish has filed several complaints with the officials on the island, as well as talking with the authorities in Savannah regarding crank phone calls, the house and kennel being broken into, as well as her disbelief that her father's death was an accident."

"And you? What do you think, Hal?" Damien asked in that soft, flinty voice Hal knew so well.

"Personally I think she's correct about her father's death not being the result of a simple burglary. As for the rest"—he shook his head —"I'm not sure. If she is involved, then pretending to be getting the calls and mentioning the break-ins could be one way of confusing the issue in an attempt to take some of the heat off herself."

"So where does that leave me?" Damien asked.

"That's the hard part," Hal admitted. "I know there's bad feelings between you and Trish, but if she's innocent, then I don't need to remind you what she's up against. If she's involved"—he spread his hands helplessly—"then she still needs help."

Damien walked back over to the chair and sat down. "Am I to assume that your department's participation in this matter can't be made known at this time?"

"Correct." Hal nodded. "I don't need to tell you that I've broken every rule in the book by discussing this with you. But I think there comes a time in every person's life when he can't always go by the rules, and in my case, this is one of those times. I only met Trish a couple of times, but I liked her. As for *our* friendship," he said, shrugging, "I don't think I have to elaborate on that."

"No, you don't," Damien said quietly, "and I appreciate what you've done. Why don't we go have some lunch and sort out the details? Trish is no fool. If I suddenly turn up out of the blue she'll know something is wrong."

"Lunch it is," Hal said as he rose to his feet. "I've also got an idea how you just might be able to 'accidentally' run into your former spouse without tipping your hand."

"Accidentally, hell!" Damien scowled. "It seems to me the best thing I could do would be to book a flight to Savannah as soon as possible."

"From what we've been able to piece together—and don't ask how we got the information—we believe Trish will soon be going to Florida."

"Florida?" Damien boomed. "Who does she know in Florida?"

"No one, as far as I know," Hal said hurriedly. He was beginning to have second thoughts about this latest development. The investigation certainly wouldn't be helped along by a jealous ex-husband erupting into the picture. "She's entered her dogs in some shows down there. If you don't like the idea I'm about to suggest, you can always sweep her off her feet and propose to her again."

Her arms laden with packages, Trish Sanders swept into the rear entrance of the interior design shop she and Millie Ames owned. She dropped her bundles into the worn leather chair in one corner of the room, which served as an office for the business, then deposited her purse in a drawer of the desk.

She ran long, slim fingers through her blond, shoulder-length hair as she walked to a

18

small counter where a hot plate kept a pot of coffee warm. As she filled a Styrofoam cup with the hot brew, a worried expression stole over her face.

Her partner stuck her head into the room. "Did you check the progress on our latest job?"

"No problem," Trish replied. "We can start work as soon as the carpenter finishes the cabinets in the file room, which should be in about three weeks." She carried her coffee over and sat down at the desk. "I brought the material you ordered from Krebs," she said, indicating the packages in the chair.

"Great. Now I can get Mrs. Tolbert off my back. She's called every day for a week. Pour me a cup of coffee and I'll join you in a sec."

Trish did as she asked, then opened the desk drawer and removed a folded piece of paper from her purse. She opened it and smoothed it out, a tiny frown creasing her forehead as she studied it.

"Why the stern look?" Millie asked as she entered the room a short time later. She walked over and stood behind Trish, her eyes scanning the sheet of paper.

"This is my itinerary, Millie, so put it some-where safe. And watch what you say—please. No one here knows that I'm going away or where. I'd like to keep it that way."

Millie took the paper, folded it, then

slipped it into the pocket of her slacks. "I'll put it in my purse later. Are you sure this is the right thing to do?"

"No, I'm not. But it's better than sitting here doing nothing," Trish said, shrugging. "Whoever this nut is, he's beginning to get to me. Night after night of crank phone calls begins to wear after a while."

Millie perched on the edge of the desk, her attractive face full of concern. "Do you think the calls have anything to do with your father's death?"

Trish shook her head. "I don't see how they could. Sergeant Decker, incompetent though he is, is convinced Dad was unfortunate enough to have surprised a burglar. And there were several homes vandalized during that two- or three-week time span."

"But don't forget, he also insinuated Uncle John was mixed up in some sort of shady dealings," Millie pointed out as she sipped her coffee.

"Well, I hope I got the message across on that point," Trish replied. "If he wasn't such a fool he wouldn't have thought anything of the kind. I'm appalled when I consider that he's the staunch defender of the law here on the island. The council must have been out of their minds when they hired him."

"I agree, but he seems to be firmly entrenched. I'm afraid we're stuck with him. However, that doesn't solve your problem."

"I'm convinced that if I get away for a few days my 'friend' will give up. At least it's worth a try. I'm determined that this jerk, whoever he is, isn't going to make me change my phone number. It's actually easier for me to leave for a while, and besides, I could use some time to myself."

Millie chewed at her bottom lip, still not convinced that Trish was doing the right thing. "Do you have everything packed? Are the dogs ready?"

Trish laughed at her pensiveness. "Yes, I'm packed, and no—the dogs still need a teeny bit of grooming. But it'll only take me a couple of hours to finish. I plan to leave around six o'clock in the morning. Anything else?" she asked, a gleam of mischief in her green eyes.

"Okay, I suppose I'm a worrywart, but I don't buy Sergeant Decker's theory that your annoying phone calls are the work of a sick mind."

"Nonsense, Millie," Trish said casually. "You've been watching too many detective movies. Even Wyatt Jamison agrees with the idea. By the time I get back everything will have settled down, and I can resume a normal life."

"I hope you're right. But taking three standard poodles on a circuit seems like an awful lot of work for one person," she argued.

Trish leaned back in her chair, a resigned expression settling over her slim features as she sought to ease her friend's concern. "Perhaps. But it's the sort of work that's relaxing. I was raised at dog shows, and every once in a while I get itchy to see old friends. A person can become lost in that world," she said, the ambiguity of the remark passing unnoticed by Millie.

CHAPTER TWO

To Trish there was something exhilarating about being up and outside before the world seemed fully awake. It was so quiet and peaceful, especially on tiny Shoppal Island, which was connected to the mainland and the city of Savannah by a causeway. She had always enjoyed the contrast between the city, with its deep historical significance, and the island, which was considered a summer vacation place for many.

The business section of the four-mile-wide, ten-mile-long strip of land boasted several businesses, including Trish and Millie's shop, a resort hotel, one excellent restaurant, and several fast-food and souvenir shops. The infamous Sergeant Decker's office was located in the same building as the tourist information center.

All in all it was a place where a person could enjoy the slow, easygoing pace of the tourist life, with the convenience of a large city close by to complete the balance.

Trish drew a deep breath of satisfaction as she hurried toward the blue van. Everything was packed and ready except for the cooler she was carrying. She wedged the igloo between two of the dog crates and then looked rather skeptically at the arrangement of crates, grooming tables, and other paraphernalia necessary for a dog show. Hopefully there wouldn't be too much rattling; she grimaced as she pulled the side door into place. An eight-hour drive with an annoying clatter in one's ear could be very unpleasant. It had been ages since she'd helped pack for a show, and this was her first time ever to do it alone.

She stood still for a moment, her hand resting on the door handle. Her gaze swept over the rambling white house where she'd been born. She loved the place, but her father's death and the tension of the last three months had mounted to such a peak, it was necessary for her to get away.

She opened the door and slid behind the wheel of the van. The engine caught on the first try, and in seconds the vehicle began to ease down the drive. She was on her way. A whole week without dreading going home in the evenings for fear the telephone would ring, a chance for several nights of uninterrupted sleep, and a brief respite from the pressures of her business.

Trish reached forward and switched on the radio. Soon the sound of music filled the close confines of the van, drawing out the sigh of relief that escaped her lips. Her enthusiasm would have been somewhat dampened had she been aware of the car that had slipped from its cover of trees and fallen in behind the van at a discreet distance.

The morning passed without incident, leaving Trish free to let her mind wander at will. She thought of the business and her decision to go into partnership with Millie. Their contrasting talents with color and ideas and their ability to blend those differences into a unique style had enabled them to present new and refreshing ideas to the design world. They'd opted to go after commercial accounts rather than private ones. Business had been shaky at first, but after a few small jobs and untold hours of back-breaking work they had managed to build a solid reputation.

She thought of Mitch Ames, whom she had dated for almost two years. He had asked her to marry him several times and she'd always refused. She had always liked Mitch, but there just hadn't been that extra something in her feelings for him. Loving and liking were worlds apart, especially when considering

25

marriage. She'd made a clean break with Mitch only a few days before her father died.

Lunch was a quick hamburger at a McDonald's. The hot midday sun made it impossible to stop longer. The heat would have been unbearable for the dogs.

Early afternoon found Trish driving through a section of Florida that had always been especially appealing to her. The gently rolling land boasted some of the finest horse farms in the country. One could become mesmerized by mile after mile of white fencing that enclosed some of the larger holdings. The beautiful animals and the lively, frolicking foals made one forget, for a moment, that this was Florida, a state noted for its citrus crop and vacation paradise.

As the afternoon wore on and the sun dipped lower in the west, Trish began to feel the strain of driving for over eight hours. She lifted one hand to the back of her neck and gently massaged her aching neck. There was one spot between her shoulder blades that was burning like a hot coal. She leaned forward and flexed the muscles of her upper back, hoping to relieve the pain.

Forty-five minutes and two wrong turns later, she pulled into the parking area in front of the motel. "Thank heavens," she muttered wearily as she reached for her purse and stepped down out of the van.

The desk clerk, an overweight young man bent on impressing the two girls working with him, informed Trish that he could find no record of her reservations.

Trish gave him an icy stare guaranteed to stop a locomotive, then leaned her forearms on the counter. "Listen, mister"—she stared at the plastic nameplate pinned to his lapel—"Hines. I have been driving for almost nine hours. I'm extremely tired and hungry. My reservations were confirmed on my credit card. We're both too old to play games, so why not give me my key and let me be on my way?"

A dull flush crept over his round face. He swallowed nervously, making his Adam's apple bob up and down. "Perhaps there's been some mistake, Miss Sanders. Let me check again."

"Yes, do that." She gave him a bright smile and then picked up a brochure listing local points of interest, thumbing through it indifferently while she waited.

In a short time Mr. Hines was back, brandishing a key as though it were the Hope diamond. "Here you are, Miss Sanders. I'm sorry for the mix-up."

"Thank you," Trish said coolly as she reached for the key.

By the time she managed to unload the dogs, their food, and her own luggage, Trish was beginning to give Millie's doubts serious thought.

I must have been crazy, she mentally berated herself as she measured food into stainless steel pans for each dog. And the worst was yet to come. There would be hours of brushing and scissoring in the morning before any of the dogs could be shown.

After finishing the feeding, she flopped down in the one armchair in the room and propped her feet up on the bed. She lit a cigarette and leaned back, inhaling deeply.

Why had she taken on such an enormous task by herself? she wondered. But the answer was simple. Some mentally deranged nut had taken it upon himself to harass her to the point that in order to retain her sanity, she had to get away for a while.

Her thoughts went back to the afternoon when her world had suddenly collapsed.

She had hurried home from the shop to fix a special dinner for her dad. He'd just returned the day before from the shows in Mexico. There'd been an automobile accident on the return trip, and Mike Tolar, one of the young assistants who worked for her father, had been killed. By comparison, John Sanders and the other young man in the car had escaped with only minor injuries. Trish knew her dad had been upset about Mike's death. She'd hoped to take his mind off the unpleasantness by serving his favorite dish, a bottle of good wine, and spending a quiet evening alone with him.

On arriving at the house and finding it empty, she had walked out to the kennel, situated at the rear of the property, her thoughts on the menu for the meal she was planning.

When she reached the kennel, she had thought it odd that the front door was standing open. It was in the low nineties, and the air conditioning was running at full speed. The shambles that greeted her upon entering the office shocked her.

"Dad?" she called out, wondering where he was. There were papers strewn all over the desk, overflowing to the floor, as well as an entire shelf of books. "Dad?" she called out again, a frown replacing her relaxed expression of only moments ago.

As she walked to the door leading to the inside runs, a small movement to her right caused Trish to glance toward the desk in time to see a sheet of paper glide to the floor. She stood frozen for what seemed like hours.

The paper landed beside the body of her father. The closed front of the old-fashioned desk he'd been so fond of had kept her from seeing him.

The coroner ruled, "Death by a gunshot wound to the right temple." John Sanders had been dead approximately two hours when Trish found him.

Since that day, a little over three months ago, hardly a night had gone by without an anonymous telephone call. They ranged from threats on her life if she didn't return the caller's property, to cruel and horrible accusations against her father. The decision to get away for a while had grown out of the tension that was turning her life into an unbelievable nightmare.

Well, she thought, shaking her head resignedly and stubbing out the remains of her cigarette. This is supposed to be a vacation, not a wake. Let's get on with it. She came to her feet and headed for the shower, stripping off her rumpled clothing on the way.

A short time later Trish stood before the mirror surveying the marked improvement in her appearance. She turned first one way and then the other, satisfying herself that the silk cream-colored shirtwaist dress hid her recent weight loss. Pleased with the results, she reached for her purse. She gave a quick glance at each of the dogs, then went on her way.

The sight that met her eyes as she turned from closing the door to her room brought a twist of amusement to her lips. She'd heard it said numerous times that dog people had gypsy blood in their veins. It had also been hinted at, rather strongly, that they were noticeably lacking when it came to common sense. Now, as Trish observed the exercise pens and the varied breeds of dogs and their weary-eyed owners and handlers scattered over the grassy area, it made it difficult not to give some credence to the accusations. But she knew that however crazy a life it seemed to an outsider, there was an excitement about showing dogs that was impossible to forget.

In order to get to the restaurant, Trish found that she had to pass through the lobby of the motel. She had almost reached the ovaled entrance to the dining room when the sound of a deep voice caught her ear. She hesitated. It couldn't be, she told herself. She glanced casually over her shoulder in the direction of the front desk . . . and immediately regretted doing so.

A pair of deep blue eyes were coolly appraising her, from her slender feet to the golden curtain of her shiny hair.

Trish lifted her chin a bit as she met the sardonic gleam lurking in that familiar gaze. She drew a deep breath in an attempt to ease the pounding of her heart as the man pushed his tall, powerful body away from the desk and walked toward her.

The years had been kind to him. The only visible difference she could see as he drew near was the scar on his temple and a notice-

31

able grimness about his face that made his already stern features sharper, more defined. There was still the same surefooted stride, the same indomitable thrust of his stubborn jaw. No, she decided in that brief moment of scrutiny, Damien St. Clair looked every bit as formidable as ever.

But then, Trish was no longer the same starry-eyed girl of twenty-two. She'd had three years to get over this man, and nothing would give her greater pleasure than to let him know it.

"Hello, Trish." He stopped just in front of her and tucked one hand in the front pocket of his dark pants. Closer inspection revealed the tiny, pulsating muscle in his jaw, which she knew was an accurate indication that he was not nearly as calm as he wished to appear.

"How are you, Damien?" she replied as politely as possible. "What brings you to this part of the country?"

"Business," he replied noncommittally, his gaze never leaving her face. He seemed to be going over her features one by one, his bold stare beginning to annoy her. "And you?"

"Dog shows," she bluntly stated. "I decided to take some time off and show my dogs."

"I see."

No, she wanted to yell at him, you don't see at all. You never did. Instead, she took a firm grip on her emotions and asked, "How's

Barb? I had a card from her on my birthday, but with one thing and another, I never found time to write back. She mentioned she was expecting a baby. Is she well?"

Damien nodded. "Everything's fine. She's getting fat and lazy. She mentioned that she'd written to you and seemed disappointed you hadn't answered."

"I've . . . been busy," she said for lack of a better excuse. And so she had, but the real reason she hadn't answered his sister's note was too personal to reveal to the intimidating man standing before her.

Damien's blue-eyed gaze raked her slim body. "It shows." And with that, he turned on his heel and walked away.

Trish's teeth bit into the inside of her bottom lip till the salty taste of blood forced her to relax. The insufferable bastard! All the animosity she'd thought buried came rushing to her mind, his arrogant, cutting remark biting into her like the sharp, searing pain of a knife. She closed her eyes momentarily, forcing herself to relax, oblivious to the curious stares of the other people in the lobby. One of those people was the thin, swarthy driver of the car that had followed the van from Georgia to Florida, and who was now pretending to study the local church directory.

Thankful for the subdued lighting that prevented curious eyes from noticing her flushed features, Trish made her way to the dining room where a smiling hostess showed her to a table.

"Would you like to order a drink before dinner?" the pleasant-faced woman asked.

"Please. A martini would be nice."

CHAPTER THREE

Trish sat sipping her drink, willing the trembling of her hands and the sensation of butterflies in her stomach to subside. She was unaware of the other diners and the soft hum of conversation going on around her.

So she'd run into Damien. So what? she lectured herself. It had been three years since the divorce, time enough for her to be able to see him without it tearing her to bits.

But why did she feel as though she'd been run over by a train? she asked herself, her vision becoming blurred as she stared at the menu. Why were all her thoughts associated with him marked by a sense of failure? Because, a tiny voice within her softly replied, you did fail, as his wife. Instead of staying and trying to work out the problems that swamped you, you chose to run.

"Trish? Oh, my dear, it is you!" a booming voice cut into the tiny, unpleasant world Trish had become lost in. She looked around, her

startled gaze finding Kate Gibbs and Josh Mc-
Donald.

John Sanders, Kate, and Josh had been dog
show friends for as long as Trish could remember. She, however, hadn't seen either of them
in a number of years. And during that time
she had married, divorced, and was now a
partner in her own business. Past accomplish-
ments or failures meant little to the older
couple. Trish was still John Sanders's little girl,
and for them that meant recounting old stories, indulging in some dog show gossip, and
prying unashamedly into Trish's present life.

"Kate! It's so good to see you." Trish smiled
as she stood and received the bone-crushing
hug the woman gave her. After extricating
herself from Kate's arms Trish turned to Josh,
who was grinning broadly. "Hello, Josh," she
said softly, his strong arms pulling her against
his broad chest for a moment.

He smelled of expensive cologne and to-
bacco, reminding Trish, for a moment, of her
dad. "I hoped, but I wasn't sure you'd be
here," she said laughingly as she stepped
back, an arm around each of them.

"Well," said Kate, "you have McDonald to
thank. We're supposed to be in Colorado, but
he has someone interested in one of those
outrageously expensive bulls he raises. So"—
she spread her hands helplessly—"you know

what happened. Since I was double-entered, we came here."

"Whatever the reason, I'm delighted," Trish assured them. "But have I missed something?" she asked, a teasing light in her eyes. "What is all this 'we' business?"

"Ah, lassie, that you have," Josh said, nodding. "This cunning and conniving woman here has finally worn down my defenses, leaving me helpless as a babe," he solemnly explained.

Trish and Kate exchanged knowing looks. "What that obnoxious devil is saying is that he's asked me to marry him. I've said yes, but there's still time to change my mind."

"Ah, Kate, me darlin'. You know you won't be doing that. Why 'tis of a broken heart from which I'd be dying." He gave her a stern look from beneath his bushy brows. "You wouldn't be wanting that on your conscience, would you?"

"Oh, you two adorable idiots. I'm so happy for you. I can't think of any two people more deserving of happiness than you. When's the big day?"

"Probably at some dog show after Best in Show," Josh dryly answered.

"Kate?" Trish looked questioningly at her. "Why are you making Josh wait so long? Some other sexy gal might snap him up while you're dragging your feet."

37

"You tell her, lass," Josh said encouragingly.

Kate stuck her nose in the air. "I'll have the two of you know a lady can't be rushed. It won't hurt him to sleep alone for another few weeks. I'm enjoying the chase."

"Shame on you, Kate. I'll add my influence, Josh. Perhaps between the two of us we can get her so tangled up in the trappings of the impending nuptials that your problems will soon be over," Trish laughingly promised.

"Any help will be appreciated, my dear, any help at all. Now, you must join us. We want to hear how you're getting on," Josh instructed her.

"But wouldn't the two of you rather be alone? I mean, you must have plans to discuss," she hedged. They were sweet and she adored them, but she much preferred to eat a quiet dinner, then return to her room. Seeing Damien had left her with little desire to visit with anyone, even old friends.

"No, we wouldn't. We've got plenty of time to think about our wedding," Kate said, backing up Josh's invitation. "Besides, a business acquaintance of Josh's is supposed to join us, so there's no reason for you to be eating alone."

After they'd chatted for a while, during which Kate expressed her regret that she hadn't been able to attend John Sanders's funeral, Josh switched the conversation to a sub-

38

ject less painful by asking Trish about her career.

Trish told them about her partnership with Millie, grateful for a break from Kate's stories of the past. "It's going great," she said eagerly. "We've finally reached the point where we can occasionally turn down a job if we don't think we'd be happy doing it. That's not to say we exercise that option very often, but it does give us a certain sense of pride. Unfortunately we've outgrown our present location, so we're in a quandary as to what to do. A larger building would be wonderful, but I'm afraid it would strap us financially."

"Are you thinking of staying on the island or moving to Savannah?" Josh asked.

"We'd like to stay on Shoppal. Besides the difference in rent, lately there have been a number of specialty shops opening on the island."

"It never hurts to have some little 'something' different than your competitors," Kate shrewdly observed, and Trish agreed. The older woman had quite a head for business and kept a close watch on the sizable fortune left her by her late husband. Nothing escaped Kate's notice, including the lack of sparkle in Trish's green eyes. "Have you been ill, Trish?" she asked in blunt fashion.

"Kate"—Josh frowned—"don't be so personal."

"Nonsense. I've known this child since she was an infant, and I see no need to stand on ceremony. Are you in some sort of trouble?" she persisted.

"No," Trish said smoothly, "there's no trouble. It's just the strain of having to take care of all the things that occurred after Dad's death. The dogs had to be sent home, plus seeing that the kennel help found new jobs with other handlers, et cetera. The only other trouble has been some crank telephone calls. Everyone assures me it's not an uncommon occurrence. So, perhaps these few days that I'm away will cause my admirer to turn his unwanted attention toward someone else."

Josh shook his head disgustedly. "The damn fool. He must have a sick mind."

"At least you aren't assuming it's a woman," Kate said sweetly.

Trish grinned at the barb, thinking that if the two of them ever did get married, it should prove an interesting relationship.

"Oh, look, Josh, there's our guest now," said Kate, nodding toward the entrance to the dining room. Trish looked up in time to see Josh wave to Damien.

Oh, no! Trish thought wildly, almost choking on her drink. This can't be happening. But it was, and she watched, stunned, as her ex-husband smiled at the hostess, nodded toward their table, then began walking toward them.

Trish sat back and waited, not sure if she should try to weather the storm and stay or excuse herself and return to her room. She had no desire to put Kate and Josh in an embarrassing situation, but she didn't know if she could bear having dinner with Damien.

The decision was taken out of her hands, however, as Damien stopped directly between her chair and the one in which Kate was sitting. "What a nice surprise," he said with infuriating calmness. "I didn't know Trish would be joining us."

"Oh?" said Kate, her dark eyes suddenly bright with curiosity. "Do the two of you know each other?"

"You could say that." Damien spoke easily as he walked around and pulled out the remaining chair. With a show of confidence that drew grudging admiration from Trish, he smiled pleasantly at Josh and Kate. "Trish and I were once married to each other," he stated, his expression unfathomable. "But I'm sure enough time has passed for us to enjoy a simple meal at the same table. Correct?"

"Certainly." Trish smiled thinly. "Haven't you heard? We thoroughly liberated women are capable of handling all sorts of embarrassing situations." Her hands beneath the table were clenched into tight fists, and she was painfully aware of Josh and Kate looking helplessly at each other.

Their relationship with her father, while friendly, hadn't gone beyond the world of dog shows. News of her graduation from college, as well as her marriage, had been met with sincere best wishes, relayed to her through her father. Once that matter was taken care of, they returned to the subject they lived and breathed—showing dogs. People's names, even that of an old friend's new son-in-law, were quickly forgotten. Trish's divorce was mentioned and the remarks had ranged from "That's too bad" to "Sorry to hear that." Life had gone on as usual.

As she watched Damien Trish was well aware that her remark hadn't pleased him. Her independence had been one of the main problems that surfaced during their marriage.

He'd wanted a wife who was willing to stay on the ranch, to act as a figurehead over a household that was run by a competent housekeeper named Rosa. After a few months of doing nothing more strenuous than preparing a meal for Damien on Rosa's day off or adding new curtains to their bedroom, Trish began to chafe against the idleness in her life. She felt smothered and frustrated.

She tried sharing her feelings with her husband, tried to explain the need for something more fulfilling than the options available to her. But Damien, completely absorbed in his love for the ranch and the unbelievable amount of time and energy it took to run it, found it unthinkable that his wife didn't share the same enthusiasm for the place he did.

"Trish?" Damien's deep voice broke into her reflective pose.

"I'm sorry." She met his enigmatic gaze. "What did you say?"

"Kate asked how many dogs you brought with you," he replied, a slight frown wrinkling his brow. As he listened to her tell Kate about the three standard poodles, Damien found time to study Trish.

From the moment he'd looked up and spotted her across the lobby, he'd found, to his surprise, that he wanted to sweep her up in his arms and take her back to the ranch, take her away from the rotten situation she was involved in. There weren't any outward changes in her appearance, other than her having lost a bit too much weight. She was still beautiful enough to make his heart miss a beat, still blessed with the graceful movements of a dancer.

It simply wasn't possible, Damien decided, that Hal's suspicions could be correct. He didn't want . . . No, he thought determinedly, he wouldn't believe that Trish was involved in something as dirty as dealing in drugs. But how the hell he was going to prove her innocence still hung heavy on his mind.

The greatest obstacle was her animosity toward him, which he'd felt as he'd walked toward her earlier. And though he felt resentment as well, nothing on earth could make him walk away from her and leave her on her own to face whatever awaited her. He had loved her once, and if he were truthful with himself, he grimly reflected as he watched her, he still did.

Trish, in spite of the apparent ease with which she was carrying on a conversation with her old friends, was intensely aware of Damien and the hard gaze pinning her. She felt as though he were making a mental note of each thing she said, carefully storing it away in his mind, as if comparing her to the younger, more inexperienced woman who had been his wife for less than two years.

By the time she had eaten a portion of the steak she'd ordered, Trish knew dessert was out of the question. Running into Damien, then being forced to sit across the table from him while she tried to eat, was about all she could handle for one evening. His presence had brought back too many memories, too many hurts for her to sit another hour or two listening to Kate's recap of all the dog-show gossip she thought Trish would appreciate.

For once in her rather boisterous and colorful life Kate raised no objections to her young friend's decision to break up the foursome, though she and Josh were quick to remind Trish that they would be around the next day if she needed them.

"I'll remind you of those carelessly spoken words in the morning when there's three poodles to brush." She smiled ruefully. She then let her green eyes come to rest on Damien, who, like Josh, had risen to his feet and was watching her with a narrow-eyed intentness that made her nervous. "Damien," she said politely, "I hope your business goes well. Give my love to Barb, and tell her that I'll be in touch."

"I'm sure she'll like that," he replied in the same polite manner.

As she made her way across the dining room Trish could feel his hard, penetrating gaze between her shoulder blades. And for a brief moment she felt like some small animal, helplessly searching for a place to hide from the keen eyes of a huge, soaring eagle.

During the short time it took her to reach the sidewalk that led to her room, Trish found herself wondering if there was a particular woman in Damien's life. In her last letter Barb had mentioned the fact that Lauren Poole was back and was making an effort to rekindle her relationship with Damien, a relationship that had died out soon after it had begun.

Now, looking back, Trish remembered the

sense of regret that news had brought. Subconsciously, she supposed her desire to keep in touch with Barb was just an unwillingness to sever her one remaining link with Damien, a link that had become so tenuous that it barely gave her tiny scraps of information about him. She knew that the main reason she hadn't answered Barb's last letter was her reluctance to admit to herself that Damien was thinking of marrying his old flame. For even though she knew she and her former husband could never live together again, Trish found it difficult to think of him taking Lauren to bed in the room where they'd made love.

When she got to her room, she took the key from her purse and reached out to insert it into the lock. But at the slightest touch of metal against metal the door swung open.

Trish frowned as she cautiously stepped inside and looked around. The dogs seemed all right, their sharp barks of greeting causing her to wonder if she'd been careless enough not to have closed the door securely. As she walked over to the crates and shushed the three excited animals, her eyes traveled about the room for some sign of vandalism, some sign of forced entry. Finding nothing, she shook her head, mentally castigating herself for her carelessness.

Convinced that it was an oversight and nothing worse, Trish changed from the shirtwaist dress into jeans and a T-shirt. Careless or not, she had three big dogs to exercise, and if she didn't get started she would never get the job done.

She walked toward the bed and the dog leashes she'd thrown down earlier. Her gaze passed over the phone, sitting between the two beds, back to the leashes in front of her, and then raced back to the phone. There was a piece of folded paper stuck beneath the plastic dial guard.

Muttering beneath her breath at the unbelievable nerve of the staff to have taken the liberty of entering her room, Trish crossed the short space to the phone, plucked the message from its secured position, then opened it, her eyes widening incredulously as she read: "Did you really think you could get away so easily? We've been watching every move you make."

The writing was almost illegible, but Trish knew, as the sensation of fear swept over her, that the crudely written note was undoubtedly for her. Suddenly, as if someone had flipped a switch, her knees began to tremble and her hands started shaking. She dropped to the edge of the bed, her eyes never looking up from the slip of paper she was still clutching.

Events from the past three months, including her father's death, raced through her mind. Three months of harassment that had given a nightmarish quality to her life, three months during which everyone but Millie acted as though she were some kind of nut for reporting the crank calls and the two times she was positive the house and kennel on Shoppal had been broken into.

Now this, she thought dazedly. She was hundreds of miles from home, and no one but Millie knew where she was. That was too much of a coincidence. She wondered if she should go home. But immediately the idea of being alone on the road, completely at the mercy of whoever had written the note, frightened her terribly. At least at the dog show she would have friends around her during the day, she consoled herself.

She thought of calling the manager and reporting that someone had broken into her room. But what could she really tell them? She could just imagine their reaction. "I've been receiving annoying telephone calls at home, and now there's this note in my room." They would probably notify the local authorities, who would get in touch with Sergeant Decker. She could almost hear him. "Miss Sanders has been under a severe strain since her father's death." She would get some sympathetic looks, some knowing ones, and a great deal of conjecture regarding her state of mind.

The restless movements of the dogs forced Trish into action. Unfortunately their world centered around their creature comforts, and at the moment they were ready to be exercised. She dropped the note on the bed, picked up a lead, then got up and walked over to the traveling cage that held Jax, the rambunctious white standard poodle puppy.

CHAPTER FOUR

Exercising was a tedious and lengthy chore, but for once Trish didn't mind. At the moment she needed time to think. She made sure the door was locked behind her and pocketed the key, her mind still whirling with this latest threat to her peace of mind.

What on earth was she going to do? she asked herself as she headed toward a large vacant area behind the motel, though no answer came readily to mind. She was frightened and she was alone, but most of all she was angry. Angry that some faceless person had singled her out to be the recipient of a succession of cruel pranks that were quickly turning her into a nervous wreck.

While she waited for Jax to sniff out every available inch of new territory and leave his scent on each bush in the area, Trish kept a watchful eye turned over her shoulder. Even though it was still early evening, she didn't feel safe, and wouldn't, till she was back in her room with the door locked.

Finally, when Jax was finished with his darting and sniffing, Trish took him back to the room and brought out his dam. Meg, sensing that all was not well with her mistress, was quick to cooperate. It occurred to Trish as she retraced her steps with Meg, and then removed Jester, the large, white male from his cage, that whoever was behind the harassment had arranged it so that only she had actually heard the voices on the telephone. They had been careful not to call her at the shop, waiting until late at night when she was in bed.

She wondered, as she went outside, what had prompted the sudden change in tactics. What had caused them to become so daring in their attempt to frighten her? Never in her entire life had she felt so vulnerable.

A whine from Jester caused Trish to look down at the large dog, his intelligent eyes watching her. She gave him a halfhearted smile and patted his muzzle. "It's all right, Jester," she murmured, "it's all right." He knew her moods well and had picked up on the turmoil going on within her.

On her trip back to her room, she had to pass a square building, which, from the sounds coming from it, housed the cooling system for the motel. Just as she turned the corner a deep growl sounded from Jester. In a flash he was between Trish and the shadow of a large man.

"Call off your dog, Trish. It's me."

Trish slumped weakly against the concrete wall, one hand gripping the leash for dear life, the other clamped around Jester's muzzle. "Stay, Jester!" she firmly commanded. She caught her breath, her angry gaze fixed on the tall, imposing figure that emerged from the shadows. "That was a stupid thing to do, Damien. If he'd slipped his leash, he'd have ripped open your arm by now," she lashed out, her voice quivering with emotion.

"Am I to deduce by the highly emotional state you're in that you'd really care if I were mauled and ripped apart by your dog?" The tone of his voice was only a shade softer than when she'd spoken to him earlier.

"I'm in no mood for jokes, Damien."

"Neither am I. But I do want to talk with you," he told her.

Trish met his gaze squarely. "We have nothing to talk about." She started to move past him, only to have him catch her arm in a firm grip.

"Do I have a choice?" she asked curtly, hating the fact that she'd run into him, and certainly not at all pleased that the touch of his hand on her arm could still send her heart racing like crazy.

"At the moment, no," Damien rasped.

They walked to Trish's room in angry silence. Once inside, she waved him to the armchair while she put Jester in his cage. "I'm sorry I don't have anything to offer you to drink, but I didn't anticipate having guests," she said over her shoulder as she straightened, then went to the bathroom to wash her hands.

"Now"—she spoke decisively as she walked over and took a seat on the edge of the bed nearest him—"what's so important that you had to frighten me half to death?"

Damien had been watching her, his elbow resting on the arm of the chair, his chin propped on his fist. He took his time answering. "Why didn't you let Barb or me know when your father died?"

The unexpectedness of the question caught Trish off balance. She dropped her gaze, her fingers unconsciously pleating the edge of the T-shirt she was wearing. She was tempted, at first, to tell him that she hadn't seen fit to apprise him or any of his family of her dad's death because it wasn't any of their business. But common courtesy and an unspoken bond that still existed between them ruled that out. In all honesty she had considered letting Barb know, then changed her mind. Later she was glad she'd made that decision. She had made it on her own for quite a while without her ex-husband or his family's help. She had been determined to continue to do so.

"I did think about it," she confessed as she looked up and met his unreadable gaze, "but things were so hectic that I just never got around to it."

"Are things still hectic for you, or have they settled down since then?" Damien asked. It seemed an innocent enough question, yet Trish was positive she heard the faint underlying hint of mockery in his steely voice.

"With the help of my friends I've managed to get my life back to normal," she returned defensively. Darn him! She wasn't in the mood to play Twenty Questions. She lifted her chin defiantly. "Is that all you wanted to talk about?"

"No," he said bluntly. "Nor do I believe you when you say you just never got around to it. What you were really afraid of is that I might come to pay my respects, isn't it? You were too damned cowardly to face me, weren't you? Instead, you chose to act like that same immature girl who ran away from our marriage three years ago."

"Go to hell, Damien," Trish lashed out, bounding to her feet in an angry move.

"Ah, no," he said determinedly. Before Trish could guess what he was doing, he reached out and grabbed her wrist, forcing her back down. "You're not running away this time. You'll hear what I have to say without resorting to one of your usual temper tantrums," he declared in a rough voice. "And while we're at it, you'll explain why you're about ten pounds underweight, and also why you reacted as though I were the Boston Strangler back there in the corridor."

Trish rubbed the red mark his tight grip had left on her wrist, her lips drawn in a line of rebellion at his treatment. At that instant she hated him. Hated him for bringing into clear focus that part of her life where the more difficult moments had been dulled by the passing of time and a concerted effort on her part to forget.

"Well?" he taunted. "I'm waiting."

"Which you may continue to do until hell freezes over," she coolly remarked as she raised her head and stared at him. "Our marriage ended three years ago. We don't owe each other anything, and I certainly don't want you in my life. I'll be leaving this town tomorrow afternoon after the show, so it's doubtful we'll even see each other again—at least I can't think of any reason for us to do so."

"Can't you?" Damien asked softly, a curious inflection creeping into his deep voice. "Perhaps I'm not content to let it drop. Perhaps seeing you after all this time has awakened a strange yearning in me, Trish. I'm reminded

55

of a beautiful girl in my arms, her body trembling with passion as she begged me to make love to her. I wonder whatever became of that girl?"

For several seconds Trish simply stared at him as something closely akin to amusement crept into her face. "Are you by any chance propositioning me?" she finally asked.

"Am I prop— What the hell gave you that idea?" Damien stormed, an uncomfortable expression settling over his rough features.

"You did," she said without the slightest regard for his pride. "Really, Damien, your routine is slipping. I can remember the time when you wouldn't be caught dead using such a line."

He opened his mouth to return the verbal volley at the exact same instant the phone rang.

"Excuse me," she murmured as she got up and walked around the bed to answer it. As she reached out to pick up the receiver, however, her hand wavered. Would it be the same muffled voice she'd been hearing nightly? With a fleeting burst of courage, she grabbed the receiver and carried it to her ear.

"Hello?"

"Trish?" said Millie. "How's it going?"

"Great," Trish replied, her voice shaky with relief.

"You sound out of breath. Have you been

working with the dogs? Did I catch you at a bad time?" Millie ran on nonstop.

"No, no, and no." Trish laughed. At some slight noise from her guest, she turned in time to see him rise to his feet and begin moving around the room. "How are things there?" she asked Millie, wishing Damien would either remain seated or get out of her room.

"Everything is quiet. Are you sure you're all right, Trish? You don't sound like yourself."

"Nonsense." Trish again tried to reassure her friend, while in the background Damien was giving an excellent imitation of Sherlock Holmes with his poking and prying. "You know where I'll be tomorrow night, so if anything occurs that you think I should know about, call me."

"Of course I will," Millie said sternly, "but I'll feel a whole lot better when you get back home."

"So will I," Trish quickly agreed. She turned, intending to keep a careful eye on Damien, only to see him bend over and pick up the note she'd left lying on the bed. "I have to go, Millie," she said quickly, then slammed down the receiver.

She took two hurried steps toward Damien, her hand outstretched. "In case you've forgotten, this is *my* room, and that piece of paper belongs to *me*. Please give it to me, it's personal."

Instead of doing as she requested, Damien held the note out of her reach and read the brief message through two or three times. When he finished, there was a frown on his face, and his eyes glittered. "Your friend doesn't sound like someone I'd like to take home to dinner," he said in an icy voice that held undertones of jealousy and possession—as if he had a right to pass judgment on her personal correspondence and her friends.

"Then there won't be any problem, Damien"—Trish glared at him—"since you won't be asked to do such a thing. Now," she said spiritedly, meeting his hard gaze with her own unflinching one, "will you give me the note and leave?"

"No." Just one word, spoken evenly and succinctly. But to Trish, who had often locked horns with Damien, that one word was enough to let her know that Mr. St. Clair—of the west Texas St. Clairs—wouldn't be leaving until he was ready. As much as it galled her to have to offer him even the slightest explanation, she honestly didn't see any other way out.

And then an idea struck her. Since Damien was determined to stick his nose in her business, why not tell him about the things that had been happening to her? She wasn't getting anywhere on her own; perhaps she could use his objectivity.

"For a moment I'd forgotten how single-minded you can be—and how rude," she said coolly. She brushed by him, stalked across the room, and sat down in the chair. Let him be uncomfortable for a while, she thought nastily. "Since you and my unknown pal seem to share a number of unflattering traits, you just might be interested in a little story I have to tell."

CHAPTER FIVE

Damien lay back against the headboard, his face impassive. He listened intently to the story Trish was telling him, but his gaze was devouring the sight of her like a starving man at a banquet. He wanted to be over her, he told himself as he listened to the sound of her voice, wanted to erase the memory of the silent agony he had endured when she had left him.

There'd been moments during the past few years when he had dreamed of the silken length of her slender body against his. He had breathlessly savored the feel of her and had ardently whispered his love, only to have the dream end and Trish's nymphlike figure disappear.

Work had become his panacea. Long hours that started before dawn and lasted way into the night. His family, in that first year after the divorce, often likened him to the devil and told him so, on more than one occasion.

What they didn't understand and what Damien had too much pride to reveal was that losing Trish had been devastating.

Eventually he recovered, outwardly, and even began to enjoy a social life—of sorts. His relationships with the different women that had come and gone in his life since Trish were conducted in such a manner that left little doubt that Damien St. Clair was as unavailable as the moon.

Little did they know that he unconsciously compared each new face to the woman he'd lost and found them sadly lacking. Now Trish was back in his life, hardly under the best of circumstances, but Damien wasn't one to question fate. He'd make the most of whatever the gods had seen fit to send him.

"So"—Trish turned her hands, palms up, in a gesture of confusion—"that about completes the story surrounding the last three months of my life. I'm totally confused and am beginning to have serious doubts regarding my sanity."

"Doubting yourself isn't going to get you anywhere," Damien told her from his stretched-out position on the bed, his arms crossed behind his head. "I am curious about one thing, though. What makes you believe your father's death didn't happen as the authorities have suggested?"

"At first I was ready to believe them. I was too stunned to do otherwise. But when I began pressing Sergeant Decker for some progress in the case, and he in turn began making noises to the effect that Dad just *might* be involved in some sort of shady dealings, I became somewhat skeptical. You must also remember that by then I was having those nightly telephone sessions with my anonymous friend. Now"—she gestured toward the note—"this. Don't you think the entire story has rather a rotten smell to it?"

Damien grinned at her down-to-earth approach to her problem. The Trish he knew, or thought he knew, would have been beside herself with fright. But not this lady, he decided, a gleam of admiration showing in his eyes. She was fighting for all she was worth. However, another part of him somehow resented this newfound maturity. Why couldn't she have shown some of that same determination when their marriage began falling apart?

"Perhaps your father *was* into something you didn't know about, Trish," Damien said quietly. "He was away from home a good deal of the time, and I'm sure the two of you led your lives, for the most part, independently of each other. People we're close to, and whom we think we know, can do strange things at different times in their lives."

"Not Dad," she said stubbornly. "He was

one of the gentlest men I've ever known. He didn't care about anything besides his dogs. There were moments when I'm not sure he even remembered I was around."

"Was he short of money?"

"No." She shook her head. "His bank balance wasn't anything outstanding, but he certainly wasn't destitute. He made a comfortable living from his profession and was very happy."

"Did he gamble?" Damien asked, trying to come up with some angle, some reason, to support her theory that John hadn't been killed by a burglar.

"Chess was his great passion, which he played with Wyatt Jamison, a neighbor. I suppose he played cards occasionally, but I can't honestly say I ever saw him do so." She looked knowingly at Damien. "I'm aware that my answers are frustrating, but I'm telling you the truth."

With ease Damien rolled toward the edge of the bed and sat up. He reached out and caught Trish's hand in a callused grip. "I'll not deny that your answers are frustrating, honey, the same as your story is. There's got to be more, a hell of a lot more that you aren't telling me or that you don't know. Which is it?"

Trish could see his eyes tracing each line of her face as he waited for her to answer him;

she saw the fire glowing in his own gaze. The sensuality of his lean, hard body seemed like a tangible force to her. It set fire to her blood and sent it coursing through her veins like molten lava.

But he was sending two different messages. One had her struggling to remember that this was Damien, the man she'd run away from three years ago; the same man who had been unyielding in his demands on her time, her life, and even her thoughts. The other message told her he couldn't quite believe her, and at the moment, this was by far the more difficult one to deal with.

"With all the many differences that seemed to spring up between us the moment we said I do, I don't recall lying as being one of them," Trish retorted stingingly.

"Not in the sense of being deliberately deceitful," Damien suggested thoughtfully as he watched her. "I think our problem was the result of rushing into a marriage before we were really ready."

"What you're really saying is that *I* wasn't ready for marriage, isn't it?" Trish murmured resentfully. "As for rushing into marriage, have you forgotten that we met when Barb and I started rooming together in college?"

"Not at all," said Damien. "But I'd hardly call those infrequent meetings a strong beginning for what later occurred between us."

Trish, in spite of the resentment she felt toward him, stared at him with an expression of mild disbelief. "Perhaps I'm an insensitive clod, but doesn't it strike you as being a little late, sitting here discussing what happened to our marriage? I mean," she said, shrugging, "it sounds remarkably like the old story of locking the barn door after the horse has escaped."

"Does it bother you, Trish?" Damien asked in the same velvet-over-steel voice she'd become accustomed to during their stormy months together. She'd never learned to master the inflexibility of that tone then, and she knew she wasn't going to do much better now.

"I've . . . gotten over it." She returned his measured gaze with her own determined one. "Should I have buried myself in sackcloth and ashes and become a recluse just because our marriage failed?" This was too much, she thought. At this particular moment in her life she had enough problems without having to listen to her ex-husband as he went back over all the old hurts and grievances.

"Well, I haven't gotten over it, dammit!" Damien exploded in a furious voice, his grip on her hand tightening significantly. "I resent the fact that eighteen months of my life were wasted because you decided you'd rather *do* something else."

"That's not the way it was at all, and you know it," Trish countered with equal force. She snatched her hand from his grasp, then rose swiftly to her feet. Damien followed suit, and in seconds they were standing with only inches separating them, glaring murderously at each other. "I was just another possession, another *thing* you brought home to your precious ranch. Another cog that would fit into the giant wheel of your organization and make it work a little smoother. No price was too great to pay for those thousands of acres of dirt and dust. You even gave up your freedom for it. And that's the mistake you seem determined to try to blame me for. Maybe you should have bought a computer, an object without feelings or needs. Better yet, you should have hired a hostess. Presiding over the dinner parties we gave was about the most strenuous thing I did for eighteen months."

"It damn well didn't have to be that way," Damien swore darkly. "Eighteen months was plenty of time for you to have a baby. But then, that would have meant giving something of yourself, wouldn't it? It would have smacked of commitment, and you couldn't stand that, could you, Trish?" The thrust of the cruel questions brought a taut grimness to his already tense face.

"I—I told you before we married that I

wanted to wait before getting pregnant," she replied in a voice not quite as steady as before. There was pain in the green depths of her eyes now, as memories she had worked hard to forget began to edge their way into her mind. Memories that she had never revealed to anyone. Not Barb or Millie, and certainly not Damien.

"Just how long did you plan on waiting?" Damien asked in a biting voice, his eyes stormy.

"I'm not sure," Trish murmured. She moved to step around him. She had to get away from the look of betrayal in his eyes, away from the hunger awakening in her body for him. But Damien wasn't to be denied. He reached out and clamped one long arm around her waist; the other one found its way behind her shoulders.

"Trish!" he muttered hoarsely as one strong hand insinuated itself beneath her chin and eased her head up so that she had no recourse but to look at him. There was a hint of compassion in the smile that played at the corners of his sensuous mouth. "Believe it or not, I didn't mean for this to happen. I thought enough time had passed that I could see you and not care. But that doesn't appear to be the case, does it?"

Trish found herself at a loss for words. Damien's admission left her with a strong sense of regret and longing that, hours before, she would have thought she could never feel.

"We all have moments when things seem to get out of hand," she said huskily against the pad of his thumb that was slowly moving back and forth across the outer edge of her bottom lip. His touch was hot and fiery, yet as soft as a feather against her skin. The dark glow of his deep blue eyes seemed to envelop her, and memories flooded into her mind; memories of lying in his arms in another place and time, of laughing with him, of feeling her blood run hot in anticipation of the moment he would take her in his arms.

"Maybe we each needed this—this exorcism of emotion. Perhaps from now on we can think of each other without there being so much resentment," she said, then realized the moment she said it that she wasn't making any sense. Forgetting Damien had proved to be *the* single most impossible task she'd ever undertaken.

"You still have that crazy habit of talking nonsense when you're nervous, don't you?" He smiled down at her. "Thinking of you has become synonymous with resenting you. I can't help but remember, and I sure as hell resent the way you tore up my life."

"Please, Damien," she said softly, "there really isn't any point to all of this. We were about as compatible as fire and ice. Let's stop torturing ourselves by dredging up all the unpleasantness."

"You're right," he said, heaving a rough sigh. "Besides, holding you in my arms is far nicer than arguing with you," he added. And Trish saw clearly the man she'd known before their lives started crumbling apart.

"That's really not what I had in mind," she said nervously as she took a step back in an attempt to remove herself from the circle of his arms.

"Too bad." Damien slowly shook his head, his gaze narrowing against the rising panic he saw reflected in her eyes. "If it was safety you wanted, then you should never have left that damned island you're so fond of."

Before the words were out of his mouth, Trish felt herself being drawn against a warmth that had slowly and steadily worked its magic against her defenses more effectively than any drug ever could have done. She felt the familiar solidness of hard thighs pressing intimately against hers, felt her breasts flattened against a chest as unyielding as granite but infinitely more pleasing.

Firm fingers gently glided over each feature of her face in an achingly familiar pattern that sent shivers of excitement racing throughout her body. His scent permeated her being, the clean, woodsy fragrance of his aftershave reminding her of the man he was and his great love for the land.

Her hands, spread against his chest in a gesture of rebuff, opened and closed in confusion as she fought the urge of desire that was sweeping over her. "Damien, this is crazy," she whispered even as she watched the slow descent of his mouth coming closer and closer.

"I know," he said softly, his lips hovering only a finger's width from hers. "It's crazy and idiotic, and I'm sure there'll be times in the near future when I'll want to break your lovely neck. But at the moment I only want to feel your mouth beneath my lips, your skin beneath my hands."

He kissed her then, one hand tangling in the hair at her nape, his other arm binding her to him as closely as if she were a part of his body. His tongue entered her mouth hungrily, darting and tasting till the world exploded in a swirl of wild, pulsating need that had her clinging to him for support. She felt the muscles of his shoulders tighten beneath her fingertips as she blindly groped for some sustaining strength in the maelstrom surrounding them.

When his lips left the petal softness of her mouth and inched their way across her cheek to her ear and then down to her throat, Trish was powerless to stop the surge of response that caused her body to melt against him like the gossamer softness of shimmering silk, obeying the slightest urgings of his hands.

"It's still there, isn't it, Trish?" The rough whisper of his voice rushed past her ear. "Holding you in my arms makes three long years of hell and an eternity of longing seem like a bad dream."

Trish opened eyes dulled with passion and met the quiet, brooding gaze of the man she'd sworn never to see again. "Oh, yes," she murmured, "it's still there, but one kiss can't wipe away the hurt we inflicted on each other, Damien. You know we can't go back to where we left off."

Almost immediately she could see the clouds of anger beginning to gather in his eyes. His arms had slackened their hold and now tightened like bands of steel around her. "You give the appearance of being a mature adult in every aspect of your life, except where your heart is concerned."

"I find it difficult to believe that after being apart for three years, then sharing one simple kiss, you would have the slightest idea what the feelings of my heart are," Trish replied in a voice not quite as steady as she would have liked.

"Unless you become limp with desire each time a man kisses you, then I would say I have an excellent idea as to what's going on in your heart." He reached out and brushed his fingers against her cheek. "Your feelings for me haven't changed at all, honey, and neither have mine for you. When you stop fighting the odds and accept it, you'll find life a lot easier to handle."

"Is that advice from one who knows?" Trish asked curiously. "Or are you trying to find a way to humiliate me?"

"If you really knew me, Trish, you wouldn't be asking that question. A man who cares for a woman, really cares, doesn't want to see that woman humiliated or hurt." He let his hands slip to her shoulders, then slowly eased them down to catch her fingers. "Life isn't always fair, is it?" he asked huskily, a glimmer of pity showing in his knowing gaze.

CHAPTER SIX

Trish's answer to this disturbing question was halted by the ringing of the telephone. She felt her entire body tensing at the shrill noise, wondering if it would be the voice that had been haunting her for so long.

"Do you want me to get it?" Damien asked, seeing the sudden stiffening of her shoulders and feeling the unconscious tightening of her fingers against his palms.

"No," she said after a moment's hesitation. "It could be Millie calling me again or . . ." She shrugged. "If it is the same person, then I'd rather know. They would probably hang up if they heard your voice."

With a sense of dread she walked around him and went toward the nightstand between the two beds. Her hand unsteady, she reached out and lifted the receiver to her ear. "Hello?"

"Are you enjoying your trip to Florida, Miss Sanders?" the muffled voice of her tormentor asked. "Did you find our little surprise when you returned from dinner?"

"Was there something in particular you wanted to talk about with me?" Trish asked briskly. Now that she had accepted the fact that they knew where she was, she found herself reacting angrily. Their harassment was deliberate. Not even Sergeant Decker could casually dismiss this latest intrusion upon her privacy.

A quick movement behind her caused Trish to turn her head just as Damien stepped up beside her. He placed a finger against his lips in a shushing gesture, then leaned down till his head was on a level with hers, his ear next to the receiver.

"Oh, we have plenty to talk about, Miss Sanders," the unknown party went on. "You have something that belongs to us and we want it back. This game we've been playing for the past few weeks is beginning to make certain people very angry. Do you get my drift?"

"No, I do not get your drift," Trish remarked resignedly. "No more than I did three months ago. And quite frankly, I'd think even a snake such as you would realize I don't have whatever it is you're looking for. You've searched my house and the kennel enough to know that I'm telling the truth."

"It's a pity you won't be more cooperative,

Miss Sanders. It would make things so much easier for everyone concerned. I'll be in touch," she was told, and then the line went dead.

Damien wasted little time taking the receiver from Trish and cradling it. He stood frowning at her, his expression one of puzzlement. "Was it the same person as before?" he asked. If she was hiding something, he thought darkly, she was doing one hell of a job. Frankly, he was becoming more and more convinced that it had been John Sanders who had something going rather than Trish.

"Yes."

"So what are we going to do about it?"

She stared pointedly at him. "We?"

"Hell, yes—we," Damien answered in a tight voice, looking at her as though doubtful of her sanity. "You've probably got no telling how many sneaky bastards hiding behind every tree in this part of the state watching you. Do you honestly think I'm about to say goodbye and walk out of this room?"

"Why not?" Trish fairly yelled at him. "Since I didn't ask you into *this* room in the first place, that is exactly what I expect you to do. As you so kindly pointed out earlier, I am a mature adult, so I would appreciate it if you would get your behind in gear and leave me alone."

"Then let me hasten to correct that erroneous statement. I'm afraid I let the passion of the moment play havoc with my thinking. What you are is crazy! Crazy as a damn loon."

Trish's lips thinned to a straight line; her green eyes flashed. She plunked her fists on her hips and was about to turn the air blue when the object of her very personal attention surprised her by turning on his heel and stalking from the room. The force with which the door was slammed caused the draperies at the windows to billow out, and left Trish with her mouth hanging open.

"Good riddance!" she yelled at the closed door. A soft whimper from Jester caused her to look at the dog, who was sitting with head cocked, his intelligent gaze resting on his red-faced mistress. "Mind your own business," Trish muttered belligerently, then swung around on her heel and began to undress.

The first thing Damien did on entering his room was to place a call to the number Hal had given him. There was barely any delay at all before his friend was on the line.

"How's it going?" he asked. "Have you been able to make contact with Trish?"

"Actually, I ran into her as I was checking into the motel this afternoon," Damien told him.

"What was her reaction?" Hal asked eagerly. "Was she surprised to see you?"

"That's a dumb question," Damien said without hesitating. "How do you think you would react if you hadn't seen your ex-husband in three years and suddenly found yourself in the same room with him?"

"Sorry," Hal replied sheepishly. "I suppose I wasn't thinking."

"I agree," Damien curtly remarked. "As a matter of fact, I believe this whole idea of Trish being your number-one suspect stinks."

"Oh?" Hal asked just a little bit curtly. "And what makes you an instant expert on the type of person who deals in narcotics?" Their friendship was too strong and they had been through too many scrapes together to worry about standing on ceremony.

"I'm not talking about just any person, I'm referring to Trish," Damien countered. "From the moment we started talking in the lobby, I could see that she's under a terrific strain. While she was at dinner someone broke into her room and left a note with some kind of veiled threats. She also got her nightly phone call. They mean business."

"Ah, my friend," Hal cautioned, "but that's part of the mystery. The authorities have only Trish's word that instances similar to what you've just mentioned have been happening to her. It strikes me as rather odd that there's never been an actual witness to any of the calls she *says* she has received."

"Wrong again, baldy," Damien quickly corrected. "I saw the note, and I also heard the telephone call. If she's putting on an act then she should get an Academy Award for her performance. Don't forget, I've lived with her. I'd stake my life on her sincerity, Hal."

"I didn't realize things had gotten that chummy between the two of you so quickly. Did you tell her why you just happened to be in Florida?"

"No, I did not, and there isn't a great deal of what I'd call peace and harmony between us, either. In fact, she just threw me out of her room. But I'm going back," Damien said determinedly. "It's obvious she's being followed. I can't just stand around and let something happen to her."

"Oh? Does Trish know she's about to have a roomie?" Hal chuckled.

"Hell, no!" Damien exclaimed. "If she had any idea she'd probably sic that nasty-tempered dog of hers on me. But don't worry, I'll get in, and I'll stay."

"Lots of luck," Hal replied. "I hope I don't need to remind you to be careful. At the moment our hands are tied, and Trish is our only bait. We'll be around, but until things become a bit more active, there really isn't a lot we can do."

"I get the picture," Damien muttered. "I would also like to add that I don't like it one damn bit. Your department's hopes of reaping spectacular headlines makes Trish fair game for anybody that wants to take a shot at her."

"Every precaution will be taken to protect her, Damien."

"Don't hand me that bull," Damien fairly shouted. "You and I both know what can happen in a situation like this. One wrong move, one lousy slipup, and it's over. By the way, my brother Nate and one of my ranch hands will get here sometime tonight. They'll be driving a blue pickup and pulling an enclosed cattle trailer. Thought I'd save you and your friends the trouble of checking them out."

The next few minutes were spent with Hal attempting to reassure Damien that it wasn't the Drug Enforcement Agency's wish that any harm befall Trish. He also gave Damien another phone number as well as the name of another agent, in case an emergency arose and Hal couldn't be reached.

Trish reached for the ashtray on the nightstand and snuffed out the cigarette she'd been smoking, then dropped back against the pillows. It was only ten-thirty, she saw as she glanced at her watch. It seemed like an eternity since she'd left home. She couldn't decide what had upset her most: meeting Damien or getting the phone call. Either way, she decided, her arrival in Florida certainly lacked the peace and quiet she'd envisioned.

Damien! Heavens, she hated to admit it, but seeing him had awakened a multitude of old aches and hurts and even some pleasant and comical memories that she'd thought long forgotten.

It was one of the latter incidents that came to mind as Trish stared at the ceiling. A smile flickered over her lips as she remembered one star-studded evening when she and Damien, thinking they had the house and grounds to themselves, had come up with the brilliant idea of going skinny-dipping in the pool.

Damien entered the pool first, then caught a laughing, protesting Trish around the ankles and toppled her into the icy water. So intent were they on inflicting harmless pranks upon each other, they were unaware of the tall, tanned figure of Nate St. Clair, Damien's brother, who had heard the noise and came out to investigate.

It was Trish, struggling to duck her much stronger husband's head beneath the water, that caught the glow of a cigarette and heard the deep chuckle of the intruder. She gave a startled squeak, pointed toward the shadowed end of the pool, and then sank to the bottom with the swiftness of a rock.

After much pleading from his sister-in-law,

who finally mustered enough courage to raise her head above the water and stare at him over the edge of the pool, and Damien's added promises of grave and premeditated punishment to his physical well-being, the mischievous Nate bade them good night and sauntered off to bed.

Trish remembered other times when Nate and Barb had pulled some innocuous prank, but it always had been out of fun and never with malicious intent. They'd accepted Trish into their family and were stunned and saddened when she and Damien parted.

Since that time she had heard fairly regularly from Barb. The two of them had even managed to meet once in Dallas while Trish was on a buying trip for the store. She hadn't seen Nate or Damien till today.

She would much rather have looked across the lobby at her former brother-in-law than Damien, Trish told herself as the touch of Damien's lips against her skin came back to haunt her. He hadn't been in the room five minutes before she was ready to fall all over him like a bowl of overcooked noodles.

She wondered at the myriad complexities of the human mind that would allow a person to know instinctively that something or someone would hurt them and yet, at the same time, allow that person to disregard those warnings and rush blindly toward a collision that would result in pain.

Her responses to the different men she'd dated since her divorce had been careful and controlled. She'd been accused of being cold. But Trish hadn't cared. That trip through an ocean of exploding stars and rushing waves of passion had been made many times by her, safe and protected in the arms of the one man who could, with equal ease, leave her shattered and torn from words spoken in anger.

No, she'd decided once the numbness of the divorce had worn off and her world had righted itself somewhat. Marriage wasn't for her. At least not in the near future, and she would certainly not have children. Perhaps one day, when the challenge of her career began to wane, she would think of making a life with someone. Someone who thought as she did and wasn't obsessed with leaving a dozen or so sons to carry on the family name.

A loud, sudden pounding on the door of her room caused Trish to jump as though she'd been shot. She jackknifed into a sitting position, her eyes wide and staring at the panel of wood as though she expected to see a monster appear.

Jester, whose crate was open, charged through the aperture, a low, guttural growl sounding deep in his chest as he positioned himself between the door and his mistress.

Without thinking, Trish reached for the telephone. At this point she didn't care what they thought about her. She was dialing the number for the front desk when she heard a familiar voice.

"Open the door, Trish, it's Damien."

A rush of relief flooded over her, causing her to drop the receiver. She jumped to her feet and rushed to open the door. "Damien?" her voice held a breathlessness, a nervous quiver as she stared at the reassuring roughness of his hard features, at the solid, unshakable height and breadth of him. "You scared me half out of my mind." She laughed weakly, then stepped back and motioned him inside.

"I'm sorry about that," Damien said as he brushed by her. "I should have phoned you first." He stopped at the foot of the first bed he came to and dropped the shaving kit and suit bag he was carrying, then turned and looked at Trish. "Has anything exciting happened while I was away?"

"Not nearly as exciting as what's about to happen if you're considering what I think you are," Trish said slowly, her green eyes swinging from the two articles on the bed to his implacable features.

CHAPTER SEVEN

"Itching for a fight, Trish?" Damien asked. There was the look of complete confidence about him, a solid strength harnessed within the massive build of his large body that had Trish silently swearing.

"What if I am?" she snapped. "I don't care to be wet-nursed, especially by you."

"Can you honestly stand there and look me in the eye and tell me that you don't need help?"

Trish took a deep breath, her shoulders rising and falling resignedly. "No," she replied slowly, "I can't. But I sure as hell wish it were anyone but you." There was resentment in her glittering green eyes as she forced herself to meet his hard gaze. She had often laughed at weird coincidences that had happened to her and to some of her friends. But this, running into Damien, was about the wildest thing that had occurred in her life.

"That's odd," Damien calmly replied as he

84

reached for the suit bag and hung it in the closet beside Trish's clothes. "At dinner you spoke so enthusiastically of being liberated. Yet here you are, swamped with indecision. That's not the way it's done. Liberation brings with it a certain definiteness of purpose, a calculated objectivity. Instead of glaring and reacting angrily because your rescuer happens to be your ex-husband and not some stranger, you should be thinking how best to use me. What does it matter that it's me or that we were once married?" He turned, his eyes alert, watching her. "In spite of the circumstances, perhaps there are some ways we can make the next few days very enjoyable for us both. Do you get my drift?"

A surge of white-hot fury swept over Trish, leaving her trembling in its wake. How dare he suggest such a thing! "Believe me," she began in a tightly controlled voice, her fists tightly clenched, "I haven't the slightest desire to go to bed with you."

"Too bad," he answered with an indifferent shrug of one broad shoulder. "Even though you seem determined to hate me, you might find that making love would remove a great deal of the tension that's built up inside you. You're headed for a breakdown, honey. Another turn of the screw and you'll find yourself flying into about a million pieces."

"Just like that, huh?" Trish stared at him,

disbelieving. "Due to my severe state of anxiety, you think a quick romp in the bed would leave me smiling like an idiot, without a care in the world?"

Damien fought to control the gleaming amusement in his eyes. "Why not? People have been using sex for years for any number of reasons. I simply wanted you to know that if you felt so inclined, I'd do my best to cooperate fully."

Trish grabbed up his shaving kit and threw it at him. "Thanks for offering your considerable talents as a lover, Damien, but the suggestion stinks. If you feel some misguided obligation to play bodyguard for me, then so be it. You're a grown man and, as you've already shown me, I can do little to stop you. Sharing my bed, however, is a different matter."

"Ah, well"—Damien grinned, his hands loosening the buttons of his shirt and shrugging it off—"you win some, you lose some. Which bed do you want?"

"This one." She indicated the one she'd been resting on earlier. It was also closest to the bathroom. She had no desire to stumble and fumble her way around in the dark in case she needed to get up during the night . . . especially with a conceited jerk sharing her room.

After making sure that the dogs were all right, Trish stalked over and dropped onto the edge of the bed, her critical gaze pinned on her ex-husband while he reached behind the heavy drape and checked the window, then assured himself that the door was securely locked.

Suddenly, to her dismay she found her heart beginning to thump crazily as she watched the way the muscles in his back and chest flowed with each move of his powerful arms. She had no trouble remembering the feel of his skin beneath her fingertips. She'd spent hours lying in his arms, rubbing her cheek against that rough growth of hair on his chest, running her fingers through it and downward, beyond where it narrowed out of sight beneath the waistband of his dark pants.

She knew every spot of arousal on his powerful body, she wistfully recalled, unconscious of the expression of longing that had slowly stolen over her features.

Damien saw it, though, as he walked to the foot of the bed assigned to him. His gaze narrowed. He'd seen it too many times to be fooled by it. So, he thought with some measure of satisfaction, he was right: she wasn't as indifferent as she would like him to believe. But what the hell would it take to get her to admit it? he wondered.

"Would you like to watch TV or read?" he said, breaking the pregnant silence hanging over them.

A slight tremor went through Trish's body at the sound of his voice. She quickly dropped her gaze, then turned and began rearranging her pillows. "It's bed for me, but don't let that stop you. The TV won't bother me."

"It's been a long day. I think I'll turn in," he said quietly.

Trish turned back the covers and smoothed the pillows for the third or fourth time, anything to keep from meeting what she knew would be open mockery in his eyes. He'd caught her gaping like a fish, caught her admiring his body as if it were the most beautiful sight in the world. Which it is, her active conscience jeered at her. Not only is seeing him without a shirt buzzing around in your mind, it's all you can do not to throw yourself into his arms.

Those disquieting thoughts caused a disgruntled Trish to punch one pillow unnecessarily hard, causing it to slip to the floor. She bent to pick it up, and as she did, the sound of a zipper and the soft rustling of clothing caused her to send a hurried look toward Damien.

He wouldn't dare!

She jerked upright as though a string were attached to her shoulders and someone had snapped it. "What on earth do you think you're doing?" she came close to yelling. She couldn't believe it. He was unconcernedly draping his pants over the back of a chair with nothing more substantial covering his body than his white cotton briefs.

Damien looked mildly puzzled, seemingly more surprised by her outburst than by the state of his dress. "I'm getting ready for bed," he told her in an infuriatingly calm voice. "And as soon as you quit scurrying around like a mouse making a nest, I'll finish."

"Finish?" Trish cried, her face becoming beet-red as the meaning hit her like a sledge-hammer. "Surely you aren't . . . I mean—"

"Oh, but I am, my darling Trish," he said stubbornly. "For most of my life I've slept in the raw." He briefly scanned the close space of the room, then looked back at her. "I seriously doubt that your friends have taken the time to install a two-way mirror. Even if they have, I refuse to let some scum make me uncomfortable."

"That's not the point, and you damn well know it," she muttered furiously as she tried in vain to stop the crazy darting of her eyes over every tanned inch of him.

There was a nasty-looking scar on his left thigh that hadn't been there before. From the size of it, it must have been a vicious wound. Had he gotten it at the same time as the one on his temple? Had he been alone when it happened? Had he suffered? "Then would

89

you please tell me the point of this ridiculous conversation?" Damien demanded.

For several speechless moments her mouth moved, but no words came out. Finally she wheeled around, her hand groping and finding the switch to the lamp. In seconds the room was in darkness. Trish crawled into bed and jerked the covers up to her ears. Her eyes were tightly closed, and the sound of Damien's deep chuckle made her grit her teeth with frustration.

Slowly the exhausting day began to take its toll on Trish. She tried to stay awake in order to mull over her anger at Damien. She wanted to nurture it, wanted to build it into an impenetrable wall that would insulate her from the desire he'd awakened in her. But her lids became leaden, and her breathing became steady as sleep eased its gentle influence into her being and gave her a brief respite from the problems facing her.

Damien was lying on the other bed listening to the soft whisper of Trish's breathing, his hands clasped behind his head as he stared into the darkness. He was aching physically for the feel of her soft, warm body in his arms, for the release of the need that had spiraled to life the moment he saw her. She still cares, he thought, mouthing the words into the darkness. Even if her lips deny it, her body tells me she still cares.

But what will be her reaction when she learns the real reason for my being in Florida? he asked himself. Would she believe that he only became involved because he wanted to help her?

These questions and many others traveled through his mind like a never-ending train till, exhausted, he fell into a restless sleep.

What on earth was that awful pounding? Trish groaned as she burrowed deeper into her pillow and pulled the sheet completely over her head. There should be a law against people making such noise.

A muffled oath, delivered with exacting force despite its low tone, caught her ear. She dug out from her cocoon of comfort in time to see Damien swing his long legs to the floor and come to his feet, dragging the sheet with him. At that particular moment Trish was reminded of the mythical rising of the Phoenix . . . only she was certain that giant creature had never begun such an auspicious occasion with a look of absolute wrath etched on its face.

"Damien," she said sharply, pushing herself up onto her elbows, a shiver of fear catching her in its grip, "be careful."

"I've got a pretty good feeling I know the identity of our caller, honey, so don't worry." He did lean forward, though, and make certain his guess was correct before removing the chain and wrenching open the door. "Was it necessary to make your appearance known before daylight?" he demanded in a tight voice. He reached over and switched on a lamp, the soft glow clearing the room of all fear.

Their guest pushed his large frame past Damien and walked into the room, his eyes blinking for a moment as they adjusted to the light. "Well, now, big brother, your note said specifically to contact you in Trish's room as soon as I got in. You really couldn't expect me to ignore such a summons, could you?"

"I suppose not," Damien grumbled. "Miracles do happen."

"Nate? Is it really you?" Trish asked. She was sitting up in bed by then, and staring openmouthed at her former brother-in-law.

"In the flesh, sweetheart," the slightly smaller version of Damien said as he turned and grinned at her. Without another word to his stern, disapproving brother, Nate sat down on the edge of Trish's bed and gave her a huge bear hug. He dropped his arms but caught one of her hands in his large ones. "How's the world treating you, squirt?" He smiled gently.

"Great," Trish answered automatically, finding herself really pleased to see this lovable idiot from her past. He'd always been a big tease, and one look at his grinning face told her he hadn't changed. "And you? Are you still trying to evade the neat little matrimonial traps Barb sets for you?"

"I'm struggling, sweetheart, I'm struggling," he solemnly replied. "I've been forced to hire five bodyguards to protect me from the hordes of women clamoring for this bod of mine."

"Are you sure it's safe for you to have left Texas?" Trish fell into his ridiculous mood without the slightest hesitation.

"Alas, no"—he dipped his head dramatically—"but when big brother tells me to get my behind in gear, I hasten to obey."

"Then let big brother acquaint you with an object called the chair, sitting on the other side of the room," Damien spoke for the first time, breaking up the happy reunion.

Nate winked broadly at Trish and stood but not before his sharp gaze took in the rumpled condition of the other bed and Damien's sheet-clad figure. He grinned wickedly. "You look like holy hell. Didn't you sleep well?"

"I slept fine, thank you," Damien snapped. For the first time in his life he found himself in the uncomfortable position of being jealous of his own brother. He resented like hell the happy little scene he'd just witnessed between Nate and Trish.

"Couldn't you at least have had breakfast

and read the paper before waking us?" Damien asked resentfully. He dropped down onto the edge of Trish's bed and reached for her cigarettes. He removed two, lit one for himself, and then handed the other one to Trish.

"Certainly I could," Nate smugly replied. "But I was too damn curious to find out why you were bunking with Trish. For a moment there, when I read your note, I thought maybe the two of you had been communicating behind my back, with the result being some sort of romantic reconciliation. But from the looks of things"—his gaze went to the other bed, then back to Damien and Trish —"I must have read more into those few words than was intended. Care to fill me in on a few details?"

"There's nothing to tell," Trish spoke up. "I've been having some problems with certain people since my father died, and Damien was kind enough to offer to stay with me last night."

"I didn't know your father had died, honey. I'm sorry," Nate said kindly. Against Trish's murmured thank-you he turned his attention toward his brother. "Is that all?"

Damien waved one hand dismissively. "You heard the lady."

"Oh, I did." Nate nodded thoughtfully. "I heard her quite well. But I hardly think either of you expects me to swallow that ridiculous tale." He rose from his chair, favoring the scowling duo with a roguish grin. "Since I'm sure the two of you have a number of things to discuss, I'll leave you to it. By the way, Damien, Charlie is asleep in your room, snoring like a foghorn. He's already chomping at the bit to get that bull from ol' Josh and hightail it back to Texas. He says Florida is too damn hot."

"Spoken like the true genius he is," Damien muttered dryly. He got up and saw Nate to the door. "I'll be over to your room in about half an hour," he said in a low tone.

"I'll be there." Nate nodded, unable to keep the fires of mischief from springing to life in his dancing blue eyes as he eyed the trailing sheet. "I hate to admit it, brother of mine, but you're slipping. A couple of years ago, nothing on earth would have kept you out of Trish's bed."

Damien hustled this latest thorn in his side out the door, his face a dark study in rage. "Unless you'd like to keep our appointment with a toothless grin spread over your disgusting face, I suggest you get the hell away from me." The door was slammed with such force, the pictures on the wall wobbled precariously.

CHAPTER EIGHT

There was a curious expression on Trish's face when Damien turned toward her, a look that made him choose his words carefully.

"If you'll tell me what has to be done with the dogs I'll help while you get dressed."

"Forget about the dogs, Damien," she said in a flat voice. "I'm perfectly capable of seeing to their needs. What I'm concerned with right now is why you, then Nate and Charlie, suddenly decided to come to Florida?"

"Really, Trish," he drawled in a bored fashion, busying himself by gathering up his discarded clothing. "I thought we'd gotten that settled."

"Did we?" she asked. "Exactly when did we have such an enlightening discussion?" There hadn't been anything of the sort, and Trish knew it. But the man pinned beneath her angry gaze was as closemouthed as a clam. "Isn't this one of your busier seasons on the ranch?

How can an operation the size of yours lose three key men and not feel the pinch?"

"The first thing any man or woman learns by the time they've reached a certain level of success, Trish, is to delegate authority. I like to think my operation would fall apart without me there to run it. But what I like to think and what actually is . . . happen to be two different things. The ranch is in very capable hands."

Trish continued to stare at him, her arms clasped around her knees. "What you're really saying is that you have no intention of telling me why I'm suddenly surrounded by St. Clairs, isn't it?"

Damien shrugged, his hard gaze never wavering. "If it makes you feel better to think I've nothing more important on my mind than annoying you, then so be it. On the other hand, I would like to point out that I had made arrangements to see Josh before I arrived in Florida. Even with your fertile imagination, don't you think you're being rather presumptuous?"

"All right, Damien," she said quietly, momentarily accepting the defeat he handed her. "I'll let the subject drop . . . for now. But just for the record, I don't believe a word you've told me. I've never been one to believe in old adages. But the one about not knowing a man until you've slept with him seems strangely appropriate now. During the time we were married I always knew when you weren't telling me the truth, just as I know you aren't now."

And for all the truth she'd gotten out of him, she could have saved her breath, Trish told herself as she showered and dressed, then began exercising her dogs.

It didn't make any sense, she thought. Damien loved that ranch more than anything in the whole world. He lived and breathed that darn dust and those infernal cows. But each question she asked went unanswered. So why couldn't she accept his arrival as a stroke of good fortune and let it go at that? Because deep down she didn't want his help. She was afraid to place herself in a position of obligation. Obligation usually brought with it a day when the balance sheets must tally. She survived the first go-around of loving Damien, but she wasn't so sure she could do as well the second time.

"Trish involved in drug smuggling?" Nate repeated in a stunned voice as he stared disbelievingly at his brother. For several seconds he appeared speechless, and then the paralysis gripping his throat loosened its hold. "It's a frame-up, a damn rotten frame-up." He got to his feet and began to pace about the room. Suddenly he swung around and looked long and hard at Damien. "And you? Do you believe Trish is guilty?"

"No, Nate." Damien slowly shook his head, a slow grin softening the harshness of his features. "I most certainly do not believe Trish is guilty. However, what you or I believe doesn't matter. Hal and his agency have been involved for months in an intensive investigation. With John Sanders dead and all evidence pointing toward Trish, he thought I should know."

"How nice of him," Nate snapped sarcastically. "I'm surprised he didn't wait until he had her handcuffed before getting in touch with you."

"Calm down," Damien said, frowning. "Without Hal taking me into his confidence there's no telling where Trish would be right now. Those damn thugs have stayed on her tail ever since she left the island. We know they're watching every move she makes."

"So Josh and his bull was nothing but a smoke screen, hmm?"

"*Is*, little brother, *is* still a smoke screen, and it has to stay that way. Trish is as suspicious as hell at finding herself surrounded by the St. Clair clan, but my hands are tied."

"What you're really saying," Nate sneered, "is that you're in cahoots with your friend Hal, and both of you are waiting for her to slip up."

"Wrong again," Damien replied shortly. "Hal knows I don't believe she's guilty. I also saw the note left in her room and heard the man's voice when he called her."

This admission seemed to take some of the fire out of Nate's eyes. All traces of his usual easygoing personality were suddenly gone. "This whole mess sounds like a giant nightmare. When I got your note, I honestly thought you and Trish had somehow gotten together again. But this"—he slowly exhaled, his broad shoulders slumped forward—"this is unbelievable."

"I know the feeling," Damien agreed. "That's the reason I asked you to come, Nate. Hal and I are friends . . . good friends. But this damn mess goes beyond friendship. He has agents who are supposed to be keeping an eye on Trish, but I wanted someone I can see, someone I can trust, someone who has her best interests at heart."

"What you're really saying is that you love her, isn't it?" Nate spoke softly, for the first time seeing a certain vulnerability in the man who had practically raised him.

"You're nosy as hell." Damien gritted, meeting the knowing gaze across the small table. "You just concentrate on helping me protect Trish, and don't read more into the situation than there really is."

"Of course," Nate said easily. He sat back in

the chair, a satisfied look on his face. "Now
. . . why don't you fill in all the details while
we're waiting for Trish."

Her reply of "It's relaxing" to Millie's question of why anyone would want to take three
standard poodles on a circuit came back to
haunt Trish. After being awakened so early by
Nate, neither she nor Damien had been able
to go back to sleep, hence her "early" arrival
at the show.

After seeing to the unloading of the van and
placing Trish's crates and tables in the center
of the grooming tent, Damien went off to find
the coffee and have a few quick words with
Nate.

It was not quite seven o'clock, Trish saw as
she glanced at her watch. But already the
show grounds, a large area adjoining a horse
farm, were bristling with activity. The white-
and-blue fencing surrounding each ring and
the red tablecloth on the judges' tables inside
each ring created a colorful display against
the freshly mowed grass.

Trish leaned against the edge of a grooming
table, her gaze touching on the striped edges
of the other grooming tent, a twin to the one
under which she was standing, then on to the
vast assortment of vehicles jockeying for the
choicest parking spots.

An expression of sadness flickered over her

face as the sights and sounds of people and dogs became a steady backdrop for her thoughts. This had been her father's life and, for the first sixteen or so years, hers as well. She felt a curious sense of oneness with him at the moment. It was as though he were watching her, knew the reason for her presence and approved.

Unfortunately, that sense of oneness with her father's memory, along with some of her initial excitement, dimmed as the minutes slipped past and Trish was forced to begin grooming the poodles.

An hour and a half later, about all she felt was a deep, burning sensation between her shoulder blades. Her right arm felt numb, and she was positive that any minute now it was going to drop off. She paused in her careful brushing of Jester and cast a resigned eye toward Jax and Meg, who were lying on their grooming tables, calmly observing the gawking spectators and the other exhibitors bustling about.

The atmosphere *was* relaxing, she kept telling herself. Unfortunately the work was something entirely different. The routine, however, hadn't varied in the slightest. And on each occasion of her departure from the sane, normal life she'd made for herself to this world of self-inflicted pain and exhaustion, she promised to commit herself to a sanatorium. Only a person with a serious mental problem would actually pay money for successive days of this!

The sound of Kate's voice broke into Trish's thoughts. She looked over her shoulder and saw the older woman working her way toward her setup.

"How's it going?" Kate asked when she reached the table, a knowing grin on her face as she, too, stared pointedly at each of the standard poodles.

"Why, it's going as nicely as a picnic in the park," Trish retorted dryly. "I was just congratulating myself on having chosen such a *relaxing* way to spend a quiet few days. Wasn't I brilliant?"

"Brilliant," Kate parroted. She reached into the large tack box and took out a pin brush and a slicker. "I swore I'd never brush another damn poodle as long as I lived, but I've learned that one should never make rash statements." She found a place for her cup of coffee and cigarettes, then looked regretfully at Trish. "Which one should I start on first?"

"That one," Trish nodded toward Jax. "Are you sure you have time?" she asked.

"Unfortunately, yes. Boxers aren't shown until three o'clock." She sprayed a light mist of coat dressing on Jax's coat and began the slow task. "Trish, my dear, have you ever considered the merits of smooth-coated chihua-huas?"

"All morning," Trish said, frowning. "I should have listened to Millie. She said I was nuts." She gave Kate a conspiratorial grin. "But I'll be darned if I let her know how right she was."

"I know the feeling. But next time, bring someone with you . . . for safety's sake as well as an extra pair of hands."

The next hour or so was spent in idle chit-chat with Kate relating her seemingly endless supply of gossip concerning people Trish knew but hadn't seen in years.

"May I ask you a question?" Kate asked after a lull in the conversation.

"Why not?" Trish replied easily, somewhat amused by the request. Kate wasn't known for her tact.

"How on earth did you let such a gorgeous hunk as Damien St. Clair get away from you? If I were fifteen years younger I'd kidnap that man and take him home with me."

"That bad, huh?" Trish laughed. She knew the older woman well enough to know that her curiosity was at an all-time high. "We parted friendly enough, Kate, as you saw at dinner. Damien is completely wrapped up in his ranch. I needed something else in my life, so"—she shrugged—"we decided that rather than end up hating each other, a divorce would best serve us both."

Very good, she told herself. If she kept repeating that ridiculous story, someday she might start believing it, though she would have to be sure and leave out how it tore her apart when she left him. Or the long nights immediately afterward when she didn't sleep or eat or do anything but mourn . . . for the death of a love that had been a living, breathing part of her.

"I suppose that's the sensible thing to do," Kate mused. "But, mercy"—she rolled her eyes—"I do believe I would have become a regular Annie Oakley to have kept that man."

"You'd better not let Josh hear you carrying on so over another man," Trish teased, hoping to get her off the subject of Damien.

"A little jealousy never hurt anyone," Kate spoke airily. "Besides, he knows I'm all talk. Chasing a man takes more energy than I'm eager to part with. Speaking of energy, why don't we take a break and go to my motor home and have a cup of coffee?"

"Sounds like a good idea," Trish agreed, then wondered if she'd been too hasty in accepting. But then Damien had urged her to act normally, to go about her usual routine. He'd also casually mentioned having given Nate a brief sketch of her problem and was confident that, between the two of them, she would be able to enjoy the day without any unpleasant incidents.

Motor home was hardly the term for the opulent coach Kate traveled in. She'd had it specially designed, from shower and tub right down to the built-in spaces for the dogs' crates.

"Nice." Trish nodded appreciatively as she slowly made her way up and down the length of the comfortable motor home. "It must have cost you a fortune."

Without hesitating Kate named a figure that brought a gasp of disbelief from Trish. "Oh, well," Kate said, shrugging, "it's only money. I may as well enjoy it while I can, because you certainly can't take it with you. How many times have you seen a hearse towing a Brinks truck?"

"Not a single one." Trish laughed, then sat in the comfortably padded booth that surrounded the table on three sides. "But then, when your time comes, I'm sure you'll be able to convince the higher beings of the wisdom of that nasty word *capitalism* . . . on a small scale, of course."

"Not a bad idea." Kate grinned and placed two steaming mugs of coffee on the table, then sat down. "You look more rested this morning. Did you sleep well?"

"Yes, I did," Trish answered, and for the first time realized that she really had gotten a good night's rest. For the first time in months she hadn't lain awake till the wee hours of the morning, worrying with the multitude of problems facing her. There were no frightening dreams of faceless people or the ceaseless ringing of the telephone. It was as though— for a while at least—she'd simply shifted the burden of worry and concern onto Damien's broad shoulders.

Trish became still, slowly sipping her coffee, with the sound of Kate's voice like a constant drone in the background. She reflected on how easily Damien had walked into her life, assessed the situation, and then assumed command. And even though it went against everything she believed in to let him do so, Trish knew that at some point she'd finally accepted that she had very little choice in the matter.

"Speaking of the devil," Kate continued like a record stuck in a groove, "here they are now."

"Who?" Trish asked, confused.

"Josh and Damien," Kate said as she got up to fill two more mugs with coffee for the two men coming in the door.

It had been a long time since Trish had been able to sit back and study Damien. Three years, in fact. There hadn't been time at dinner last night or later in her room. On both occasions she had been too confused by the shock of seeing him and had had a difficult time controlling the feelings for him that had lain dormant for so long.

Now the shock had been reduced to an aching awareness, and her feelings where he was concerned were demanding a reckoning. For one brief moment, as she watched him smile and talk with Kate and then turn and look at her, Trish wondered what was the lesser of the two evils facing her: unbelievable harassment from the unknown persons making her life a living hell, or the kind of hell that came when two people seemed bent on destroying each other in the name of love.

Damien slid into the booth beside her, his long, hard thigh pressed against her softer one. "You're looking unusually thoughtful," he said to her softly, his blue eyes sharp and probing as they scanned her face, then lingered on the softness of her lips. "Did Nate and Charlie slip up?"

"No, they've been very attentive . . . at a distance," Trish quickly assured him, then lapsed into an uncomfortable silence, finding that his gaze was making her inexplicably uncomfortable. This condition caused a ripple of resentment to flow through her. Don't be such a wimp, she lectured herself. He's your ex-husband, for heaven's sake, not some monster. Relax; treat him the same as you would any other man. "I'm afraid they are going to be terribly bored before the day is done."

Damien grinned. "I think *amazed* is a better word. They can't get over all the fuss and bother involved in showing dogs."

"Most people are a little amazed by all this." Trish chuckled.

Kate and Josh joined them then, and the merits and price of one of Josh's bulls became the topic of conversation.

When Trish heard the amount of money involved, she turned startled eyes on Damien. "You're actually considering paying such a price for a . . . a bull?"

He laughed at her look of astonishment. "Of course. I'm getting a fair deal."

Trish swung her gaze to Josh. "I'm sure I must have missed some important feature regarding this amazing animal. For example, gold hooves? Perhaps he sires calves that speak?"

"At least," Josh said, laughing. "And the gold on their tiny hooves doesn't appear until they are about three months old."

"Well"—Trish shook her head and sighed resignedly—"to each his own. But if I were ever weak-minded enough to pay such an exorbitant price for an animal, I'd hire two men to personally attend him . . . one to fan him and the other to play soft music to keep him calm. There is one thing about this discussion that gives me some comfort, though."

"I'd be interested to hear it." Damien smiled.

"It only goes to prove that dog people aren't the only ones with a screw loose."

"I couldn't have put it better myself, Trish," Kate joined in, and immediately became involved in an argument with Josh regarding the merits of showing dogs as opposed to paying exorbitant prices for bulls.

"The thought of those two being married to each other is rather mind-boggling, isn't it?" Damien said awhile later as he and Trish made their way back to her setup.

"And how," Trish agreed. "Yet I think their arguments are good. They're each stubborn as heck and not afraid to stand their ground if they really believe in something."

"Arguments have been known to be a very destructive force within a marriage, though. Don't you agree?"

A painful look flickered across Trish's face as the ambiguity of his remark reminded her of their own marriage and the endless battles that eventually destroyed it. "It makes one wonder, doesn't it?"

"About what?" Damien asked softly as one long arm found its way to her shoulders.

"About what happens to the plans two people make before they marry, the dreams they have, the unwitting promises that go along with those plans and dreams. Every hope, every one of those dreams is turned toward their wedding day. That day comes in a flurry of excitement. The honeymoon is a period of fantasy, and then comes the reality. I hope Kate and Josh are smart enough to face the reality before the honeymoon. It could go a long way toward saving them from growing to hate each other."

"Is that what you feel for me, Trish?" Damien asked close to her ear, his breath fanning her cheek.

Trish stared straight ahead, silently praying the ground would open up and swallow this very large pain in the buns walking beside her.

"Don't flatter yourself, Damien," she retorted calmly. "I've had more on my mind these last three years than nourishing hatred for you." She lifted one shoulder indifferently.

"Hoping to mark my tough hide, Trish?" he grated.

"Not in the least," she countered bravely, "merely stating a fact. I think each of us left enough marks on the other when we were married, don't you?"

"Indeed not," Damien drawled, "I'm descended from a long line of St. Clairs, who were cursed with enormous masochistic tendencies. I enjoyed our brief marriage so

111

much, I'd leap at the chance to marry you again."

Trish stopped dead in her tracks and raised startled eyes to meet his dancing ones. She'd been both insulted and complimented, and at the moment she wasn't certain how she should respond, with outraged indignation or the delightful release of acquainting his granite-hard head with a two-by-four. "You're crazy!" she hissed instead, then scurried like a timid mouse for the sanctuary of her setup. He was getting to her, slowly but irrevocably inching his way back into her heart. She had to stop him, she told herself, before he destroyed her.

Her hands were shaking as she took Jax from his crate, placed his front feet on the edge of the grooming table, then patted the center of the table, a signal for him to spring onto the surface. Just as he did so, Trish caught sight of a small, single sheet of white paper weighted down by the bottle of coat conditioner.

She picked it up, her eyes quickly following the blunt message: "How would you like to spend the rest of your vacation in the hospital? Unless we get what belongs to us, that's exactly what's going to happen to you. We'll be in touch."

Damien took one look at her face as he approached the setup and frowned. "What's wrong?"

"This," Trish murmured as she handed him the note. "I found it on the grooming table."

He read the note through twice, his muttered "God damn it!" revealing the depth of his rage. His large fist crushed the slip of paper as he swung around to scan the crowd. "I'll wring Nate's neck for this slipup."

"Don't be ridiculous," Trish cried. "Nate has no control over these idiots. In case you haven't noticed, there're a lot of people milling around. How can he possibly watch everyone?" Damien turned and stared at her, by his very silence accepting the logic of her words while chafing against the invisible boundaries cast around them by the unknown enemy.

Suddenly Trish found herself feeling sorry for this large, angry man who was trying to protect her. He was accustomed to having his orders obeyed. He snapped his fingers, and men jumped to do his bidding. She could well imagine the frustration holding him in its grip. She'd been caught up in the same senseless battle for the last few months.

CHAPTER NINE

The last-minute preparations necessary before taking a dog into the ring helped to keep Trish from dwelling on the fact that even in a huge crowd of people she wasn't safe. She'd always found that period of time just prior to showing her dogs to be especially tense, and as she hurried between the three tables, touching up a topknot here, fluffing a pompom there, the familiar sensation of butterflies had her stomach in knots.

She also knew from experience that it was a time when a professional handler or exhibitor wasn't at his best in terms of conversation. It was impossible to answer the many questions asked by curious visitors when one was working like a fiend against the clock.

Unfortunately the visitors weren't her immediate problem today. Trish frowned as she worked. She was being slowly but surely driven out of her mind by the incessant arguing of Damien and his brother, each determined to prove a point.

She threw a disgusted look toward Damien and Nate, at the moment wanting nothing more than for them to be whisked back to Texas and to the backside of their ranch.

After finishing some light scissoring on Jester's coat she turned, finding her path to Meg's table blocked by the large presence of her ex-husband, who was talking a mile a minute.

"Move," Trish snapped loudly, her anger glinting in her green eyes.

Damien interrupted his heated monologue long enough to turn and look searchingly at her. "Is something wrong?" he asked worriedly.

"Yes"—she glared at him, the one word closely resembling a snarl—"in spite of the efforts of some weird characters intent on doing me bodily harm and your equally infuriating intention of protecting me, I would still like to show my dogs."

"No kidding," Damien retorted with equal sarcasm. "I thought we were standing under this damn grooming tent in hundred-degree weather just for the hell of it."

"I'm beginning to think that's exactly what we're doing."

"Would you mind telling me exactly what is preventing you from showing your dogs?"

"You are," Trish declared furiously, "along

with your brother and your trusty sidekick. I can't move without bumping into you. To put it bluntly, Damien, get the hell out of my way."

"Believe me, madam, at the moment nothing would give me greater pleasure. However, were I to do what you so graciously suggest, some sneaky bastard would probably throttle you. Can you possibly absorb such a sobering thought into that thick head of yours?"

"Kindly leave the thickness of my head out of this discussion, Mr. St. Clair," she countered icily. "As for being throttled, I'm beginning to think it far more humane than being forced to listen to your rantings and ravings."

They stood glowering at each other, each determined to have their way, each refusing to budge an inch. Nate and Charlie, unaccustomed to seeing Damien told off, watched the display of tempers with open amusement. After quickly deciding that an impasse had been reached, Nate stepped forward.

"I think what Trish means, Damien, is that she would like some space," he said smoothly. "Why don't we move our discussion over there by that tree? That way we can keep an eye on her, and she can have room enough to finish grooming her dogs."

"Thank you, Nate." Trish smiled coolly. "It's refreshing to know that at least one

116

member of the St. Clair family is sensitive to the feelings of another person."

"Sensitive?" Damien spat the word out. "You have about as much sensitivity as a damn brier patch. I've never met a nastier-tempered, flintier-eyed—"

"That ain't no way to talk to a lady, Damien," the solemn-faced, seldom-speaking Charlie chimed in. He gave Damien a hard look, then turned to Trish, his leathery features softening. "You go right ahead and finish whatever it is that you have to do to them poor dogs, honey. I'll keep the boys out of your way."

Trish blinked at how easily Charlie had taken control, and was further amazed when her particular fire-eating "boy" turned and stalked off. "Thanks, Charlie," she murmured as the older man started past her.

"Damien is a mite bothered now, Trish. I wouldn't ride him so hard if I were you. He can be real nasty when he's riled."

Don't ride Damien so hard? Trish thought with a groan as all three men headed for the spreading limbs of a large tree several feet beyond the tent. What a laugh! What about the way he was riding her? she was tempted to shout after them. They'd been together for less than twenty-four hours, and there'd been barely a kind word spoken between them. Don't ride him hard, indeed!

"I wonder what the penalty in Florida is for willful, gleeful, and absolutely premeditated murder?" she muttered as she turned back to the waiting dogs.

From the minute Trish entered the ring with Jax, she wanted to choke him. He bounced like a rubber ball in true puppy fashion, grabbed the leash in his mouth, and tried to climb into her pocket for the liver she was using as bait. Every conceivable trick in the book was tried by the unruly rake.

Trish caught sight of her St. Clair entourage standing with Kate at ringside as she was attempting to gait Jax around the ring, their grins taking some of the sting out of his performance. When the embarrassing exhibition was over, she was surprised to see that the judge had placed Jax second in the class of four.

"You stupid mutt," she muttered as she waited for the ribbon and tried to dodge a deluge of sloppy kisses from the witless wonder she was holding on a leash. "If you'd behaved you might have placed first."

After the class was dismissed, Trish hurried back to the setup, nervously fluffing and combing on Meg's already perfectly groomed coat. Nate followed her, a frown on his face as he studied the point schedule in the front of the catalog.

"I heard you and Kate talking about points a little while ago," he said to Trish. "How does a dog pick up points?"

Trish gave him a sympathetic grin. "I'll try to explain the basics, but don't feel bad if it all sounds like Greek; it would be easier if you knew something about dog shows. A dog must have fifteen points to be awarded his championship. At least six of those points—or two three-point majors—must be awarded under different judges at different shows."

"How do you know how many points are in each show?" Nate asked.

"The number of points is arrived at by the number of dogs entered and shown in a particular breed. The larger the entry, the more a dog may win, to a maximum of five points for any one show. To insure that a dog is deserving of a championship, it must obtain two major wins."

When they took their place in the ring, Trish stacked Meg, who, unlike her bouncing offspring, was a joy to handle. The judge paused in his first examination of the dogs when he came to Meg, and then moved on down the line.

After going over each entry individually and gaiting them, the judge motioned them all around for the final time. Trish gave her dog plenty of lead, and Meg moved out. Without the slightest hesitation the judge placed Meg first.

Trish's happiness at his decision was clear from the smile that came readily to her face. What was even nicer was the round of applause from the gallery.

After accepting the blue ribbon with a hurried thank-you to the judge, Trish quickly made her way out of the ring and to a waiting, smiling Kate. "I hope you don't mind showing her for Best Breed."

"Not at all." Kate laughed. "But, if it was the puppy I might have some reservations."

"I know what you mean," floated over Trish's shoulder as she raced to get Jester.

Trish had had some misgivings about whether or not Jester would show well, considering it had been several months since his last outing and that her father had always handled him. Her fears proved unfounded, however, for Jester hadn't forgotten a thing. He moved around the ring like a trooper, his tremendous drive and superb gait a pleasure to watch.

As she waited for the other dogs to go through their paces, Trish tried to calm the nervous feeling gnawing at her. Having Jester win Best Variety would go a long way toward making an otherwise miserable day seem brighter.

Apparently the gods decided to smile upon

her. For not only did Jester win Best Variety, but Meg went Best of Winners. On exiting the ring Trish was congratulated by a number of people, including Kate, who had done an excellent job of handling the bitch.

Even Damien suddenly materializing beside Trish, and dropping an arm around her shoulders and pulling her close, failed to put a damper on the event. Her warm response to his touch brought a gleam of satisfaction to his eyes.

Kate stood back, somewhat surprised, her watchful eyes taking in each move, each gesture, a thoughtful expression flitting across her face. "You've only got about ten minutes until the Groups," she reluctantly reminded Trish.

It was as though Kate's voice brought back reality and the harshness it entailed. Trish stepped out of the circle of Damien's arm, pretending a nonchalance she was far from feeling. It had been the most natural thing in the world to feel his body close to hers, to hear his murmured congratulations in her ear. It had somehow made her victory complete.

She studiously avoided eye contact with Damien for fear he would see the hunger that had sprung to life so effortlessly within her, making her forget, for a moment, that this was a man she could not allow herself to become involved with. Not again. It was a strange and eerie feeling being thrust into such a close relationship with the one person capable of hurting her. Even more difficult was trying to maintain an air of indifference toward him. Having Damien for a constant companion was proving to be nearly as unsettling as being pursued by the unknown men intent on reducing her life to a constant hell.

Jester didn't win the Group as she'd hoped; nevertheless, Trish congratulated the handler of the dalmatian that did win and made her way out of the ring.

"That judge must have owed somebody something," Kate remarked disgustedly as they made their way back to the setup. "You should have had that Group."

"I agree." Trish shrugged. "But I can't complain, I've had a nice day. I would like to send the dear man copies of several breed standards, though. It's obvious he needs them."

They had walked on a little farther when Trish suddenly looked around. "Where is Damien?"

"Don't worry," the older woman dryly remarked. "The man you're supposed not to care for is over there with Josh and Nate." Kate nodded in the direction of the grooming tent. "It's funny, but I'm having one heck of a time reminding myself that the two of you are divorced."

"Nonsense, Kate," Trish calmly answered.

"You and Josh are so in love, you look at everyone else in the same light. He came to talk business with Josh, and I was here. It would be silly for us to try to ignore each other."

"What a lot of dribble." Kate snorted. "If that's the story you're putting out then it's okay with me. But please don't expect me to believe such an incredible tale."

Trish didn't pursue the matter and devoutly hoped Kate wouldn't. She had no desire to get into a lengthy discussion regarding her relationship with Damien. She was having enough trouble coping with her own thoughts regarding the subject.

Unfortunately Kate, with her own unique way of starting trouble, lost little time in getting Trish involved in yet another argument with Damien. "Why don't the two of you join us for dinner?" she asked Trish as soon as they were back at the setup and there was a lull in the conversation. "Josh's nephew will be with us, and I'm sure he'd rather look at your pretty face than my ugly mug."

"Thanks, Kate," Damien spoke up before Trish had time to answer, "but I have other plans for this evening, and I think it would be best if Trish got to bed early."

For several seconds Trish remained silent. Her hands were busy with brushing and wrapping Jester's topknot and ears, but her anger had been thrust into overdrive and was

123

rapidly consuming her. She raised cold, defiant eyes toward Damien, her lips compressed into a straight, rigid line.

"Dinner with you and Josh sounds great, Kate," she said determinedly. "I should be through here and on my way in another thirty minutes." She did some quick calculations regarding the length of time it would take her to drive to the small town where the show would be held the next day. "Why don't I meet you around seven thirty?"

"Seven thirty it is," Kate quickly agreed, her amused gaze darting back and forth from Damien to Trish. "The location of the only decent restaurant hasn't changed, so we'll be saved the problem of quibbling over where to eat. Do you remember how to get there from the motel?"

"I remember," Trish said, unconcerned. She finished with Jester and moved on to Meg, ignoring the flinty stare emanating from Damien. The moment Kate and Josh left, she whirled around and faced him, her green eyes flashing. "Let's get one thing straight, Mr. St. Clair," she threw at him. "If I wanted a social secretary I would hire one. *I* decide where I will go and with whom . . . not you." She was forced to pause and take a deep breath, her anger causing her breathing to become shallow. "I have a legal document, signed by each of us, clearly stating that you and I are no longer man and wife. In other words, Damien, you have no say in what I do. If I choose to walk naked down the interstate with a basket of fruit on my head and a gaggle of geese at my heels, it's no concern of yours!"

"Damn, Trish!" Nate burst out, ready to choke on his laughter. "If and when you do decide to pull off that particular stunt, let me know. It should cause quite a stir."

"Not nearly the stir that I'm going to cause when I beat the flaming hell out of you," Damien roared at his brother. He looked from Trish to Nate, barely able to contain himself. "Not only am I saddled with a brother who acts and sounds like a damn fool, I also am cursed with a wife who is doing everything within her power to make herself an available target for somebody with a mind as screwed up as a broken spring!"

"Ex-wife!" Trish informed him in an imperious voice. "Kindly remember that in the future. I resent being constantly reminded of the mistake I made in thinking you were human."

Damien's face turned a deep red beneath the tanned skin as her remarks pierced his tough hide. "Has anyone ever told you that griping doesn't become you?" he snapped, then swung around to his grinning brother. "If you can manage to stop grinning like the

125

fool you are, then pick up Charlie and go take a look at that bull I'm interested in."

"I'll be happy to." Nate threw his shoulders back and sketched a brief salute that had Trish biting her lip to keep from laughing. "It's always such a pleasure working with you, big brother. You're such a calm, quiet person, and you always ask for one's help in such a courteous fashion."

Trish watched Nate as he walked toward his car and was reminded of the number of times she'd seen that same stride leaving her or coming toward her. But it had been Damien then, a Damien who had brought the bursting light of his love into her heart, leaving her breathless and, at times, crying with the incredible wonder of it all.

"I'm sorry if I spoke out of line," Damien said quietly, finally breaking the gentle moment of reverie that had stolen over her.

Trish turned her head and looked up into his eyes, her own gaze strangely softened by her thoughts. "It doesn't matter, Damien. I suppose I overreacted." She smiled. "I'm afraid I don't take kindly to being told what to do."

A faint glimmer of humor sparkled in the depths of his eyes as he stared down at her. "And we both know I'm not the most diplomatic person in the world when it comes to people I care about and their welfare."

"Nonsense," Trish said teasingly. "Didn't you hear Nate? You're the epitome of Mr. Smooth. You have such a *gentle* manner about you when you *request* someone to do something, it almost takes their breath away."

He did smile then, and the effect on Trish was indeed breathtaking. His blue eyes became warm pools of entrapment that left her feeling as though the hard ground she was standing on had suddenly become a soft, undulating carpet, ready to send her gliding into his arms.

"Even though you don't want to hear it, Trish, I still love you. I haven't forgotten a single moment with you, the good ones or the bad ones," he spoke in a husky whisper. "Sometimes, late in the evening, I saddle a horse and ride till I come to that gnarled old tree beside the creek where we used to go. I sit there, my back against the tree and my eyes on the sunset. But instead of seeing the colors slowly disappearing before my eyes, I see you, smiling, happy, lying warm and soft against me and tempting me with your body. How about you, Trish? Do you ever take time out to remember?"

"Oh, yes," she said, her voice sad, "I remember. But unlike you, it's the hurt, the misunderstandings that haunt me. It's taken a long time for the wounds to heal, Damien, and I'm not anxious to reopen them."

"What you're really saying is that you don't want to become involved with me, isn't it?" he asked harshly.

"Yes, it is. Resurrecting old loves is a big mistake." But in her heart there was a different answer, one that she was helpless to control. She knew that becoming involved with Damien again was as inevitable as taking her next breath.

"So is denying existing loves," he countered silkily. "By the way, I'll be taking you to dinner, so you can forget whatever notions you might have of spending the evening flirting with Josh's nephew."

CHAPTER TEN

The trip to the next show was a tense one. Trish had hoped to be alone for at least that short period of time, but Damien wouldn't hear of it.

As she stepped hurriedly from the shower and reached for a towel, she shook her head with annoyance. She and Damien were to be roommates again, and quite probably that would continue for the length of her stay in Florida, she thought resignedly. That fact had been revealed to her upon their arrival and during their exchange of words in front of the motel when he'd asked her about her reservations.

"Naturally I have reservations here for only one night," she told him. "Tomorrow I'll be going on to the next show. Why?"

"Because I'm giving your room to Nate. You can stay with me."

"Oh, really?" Trish bristled.

"Really," Damien mimicked.

"I don't remember us making any such plans. Staying with you is out of the question."

"Why? Are you afraid of what it might lead to?" he asked mockingly.

"Believe it or not, Damien"—she smiled coolly—"I can manage to be around you for a considerable length of time without flinging myself into your arms. All I want at this stage of our little charade is one night of peace and quiet, which I'm not likely to get if we share a room."

"I really hate to disappoint you, honey," he replied sarcastically, "but we will share a room. As for peace and quiet, you'll have to work that out for yourself." And with those sharp words he'd gotten out of the van and strode into the motel office.

"And here we are, America's ideal couple." Trish smirked as she finished drying herself and then slipped into fresh underwear. There must be some way to outmaneuver him, she told herself as she drew on a pair of light green slacks and a matching short-sleeved crocheted sweater.

But you feel safer than you have in months, don't you? her irritating conscience prodded her. You've had an entire day, barring the incident with the note, in which you've relaxed and become a normal person. Can you honestly deny that without Damien's presence you could have accomplished such a thing?

"No, I can't deny it," she whispered on a long sigh as she stared at her reflection in the wide mirror above the dressing table, "but it hurts to admit it, it hurts so very bad."

There was a certain grimness in Damien's face as he paced about his friend's motel room, and it left Hal in little doubt of his displeasure. "I think your reasoning stinks," Damien muttered as he made one final sweep of the room, then dropped into a chair.

"Has it occurred to you that the reason you think that is because Trish is involved?" Hal quietly asked.

"Hell, yes, it's occurred to me . . . just as it would occur to you if the situation was reversed. All those rules and regulations we were taught years ago, and which you still live by, might be fine if you're dealing with someone you don't know. But in this instance we're dealing with Trish, and I don't give a goddamn for your rules or regulations."

"We've got to do it this way, Damien," Hal continued patiently. He knew his suggestion was a pushy one, but then, they weren't dealing with a group of little old ladies in tennis shoes. The organization behind the harassment aimed at Trish couldn't be less concerned about what happened to her.

"If we move in now and surround her with an army of agents, we'll never get to the bottom of this thing. I'll be the first to admit that our chances of having a serious impact on drug smuggling with this one bust are nil. But however many smugglers we put out of commission, then that's just a few less for us to have to deal with in the future."

"Give me a time frame, Hal," Damien said, scowling. "I don't like having to run my life by someone else's whims, even if they happen to be your whims."

"We're not selling cattle or repairing fences on your ranch or checking the production sheet on one of your oil wells, Damien," Hal told him. "We're dealing with criminals of the worst kind, and we're trying to protect a human life. Time frames don't mean anything in this business."

"I'm not sure how much longer I can fool Trish. She's as suspicious as hell already, especially with Nate and Charlie arriving on the scene. I've pacified her for the moment by telling her that I've mentioned to Nate that she's having a few problems with crank phone calls. Unfortunately that doesn't keep her from thinking I'm losing my mind."

"That shouldn't bother you." Hal laughed. "I've never known you to be concerned with what other people think."

"Usually I'm not," Damien readily admitted.

"But, as you said earlier, this is Trish. Correct?"

"Correct."

"I've been giving that particular problem some thought, Damien. How *will* you tell Trish about your involvement?"

"That's a question I've been asking myself ever since you visited me in Texas. No matter what I say, she's bound to resent the fact that I knew she was a suspect and failed to tell her."

"But from the beginning you haven't thought her guilty, have you?"

"No, especially not after hearing her story," Damien said slowly. He got to his feet and began moving toward the door. "Knowing Trish as I do, though, she'll probably hate my guts for deceiving her."

"I'm sorry," Hal sympathized. "But I'm afraid there's little I can do to help you at the moment. And about all you can do is stick as close to her as you would if you were her husband. Who's with her now?"

"I left Nate sitting by the pool, directly across from the door to our room. Trish is getting dressed to go out to dinner with Josh and Kate."

"Be careful," Hal cautioned as the door slammed shut.

Sean, Josh's nephew, wasn't at all the youthful teenager Trish had assumed him to be. He was fresh out of college, reasonably good-looking, and "working his way up" in one of his uncle's banks. After meeting Trish and immediately deciding that she was just the sort of "older woman" he needed to round out his life, he marshaled together the forces of what he considered his irresistible charm and blasted her with the full barrage.

If she even hinted that she wanted a cigarette, he was ready with his lighter. Her request for each additional margarita was filled so quickly, Trish was tempted to laugh. When she accidently let her napkin slide off her lap, she almost bumped heads with her young swain as he swooped to retrieve it for her. He clucked over her like a broody hen with one baby chick, either blissfully ignorant of or stupidly ignoring Damien's stormy gaze.

It occurred to Trish, as she struggled to divide her attention between Sean on her left and Damien on her right, that this was the first time she'd ever seen Damien openly jealous of another man. There had sometimes been remarks tossed back and forth between him and Nate when the latter showed her too much attention. But Trish had never thought anything about it, simply accepting it as another facet of the relationship between the two brothers.

But there was nothing at all brotherly in the way he was acting now, she told herself as the evening wore on and she felt the tension building. It was as though they'd never been separated, so attuned was she to his mood. She could see the tiny muscle in his cheek continuously throbbing, an unmistakable sign that his anger was increasing, and the curt manner in which he answered any remark addressed to him left little doubt as to how he was feeling.

Perhaps it was the incredible strain of having a babbling idiot on one side of her and a flinty-eyed maniac on the other side that caused Trish to have such a sudden and insatiable craving for margaritas, she reasoned as she deliberately ignored Damien's sharply indrawn breath of exasperation and ordered another drink.

As she'd expected, Sean didn't wait for the waitress but went himself to get her drink. "You do realize that you're getting royally drunk, don't you?" Damien remarked sourly in her ear. "I would also like to remind you that you can't carry your liquor worth a damn."

Trish turned and focused her green eyes on him, stung by the open displeasure in his face. "I can carry my liquor like a rock," she haughtily informed him.

"Like a sinking rock," he murmured

gruffly, then effectively silenced her by leaning toward her and dropped a quick kiss on her surprised lips. "I must be stupid for trying to stop you, considering how passionate you get when you're slightly tipsy. I remember one rather remarkable occasion when you made my blood run hot with your own very special performance of Salomé. Then there was the time—"

"Shut up!" Trish hissed as she gave a frantic glance down the length of the long table. Luckily, everyone was listening to Josh, who was telling some wildly funny joke. Trish turned her attention back to the asinine smirk on Damien's face. "Isn't anything sacred to you?" she demanded loftily.

"Oh, yes," he answered just as fervently, his gaze and the suggestion of intimacy it carried leaving her flustered and unsure of herself. "I treasure those memories more than anything else I can think of."

A dark-clad arm sliced down between them, saving Trish from having to react to Damien's words. "I had the bartender mix that one exactly like the others," Sean proudly announced as he withdrew his chair and sat down next to Trish. Not content just to be seated next to her, he turned in his chair so that he was facing her rather than Nate, who was directly across the table from him.

"I've had about all I can take from that pimply-faced kid," Damien grated into Trish's other ear. "If you can't get rid of him I'll do it myself."

For the next five minutes Trish didn't know whether to laugh or cry. She felt like the meat in a sandwich, the mortar between two bricks, a bone being tugged between two snarling dogs. She dared not look left or right. Instead she stared straight ahead, not a muscle in her body moving, except her arm, which, like a mechanical lever, brought her glass to her lips and then replaced it on the table. Up and down . . . straight ahead!

It wasn't until the image of Kate, who was sitting across from Trish, suddenly became blurry that it occurred to her that she was well and truly soused. Ignoring Sean's continued monologue and Damien's narrowed gaze, she abruptly murmured, "Excuse me," then pushed back her chair and rose to her feet. She turned and began making her way toward the ladies' room.

Just as she reached for the doorknob Kate appeared beside her. "Anything I can do?" her old friend asked, her eyes gleaming with laughter.

"Yes!" Trish snapped as they entered the small lounge. "Call me a taxi."

"What on earth for? Most women in that room out there would give their right arm to be in your position. You have two men ready to come to blows for a moment of your time."

"Th-then you have my permission to make an announcement that any and all the women present are welcome to both men. I'm si-sick of them," Trish announced haltingly as she edged her way to one of three fragile-looking chairs in front of the narrow vanity and mirror and sat down.

"Is there any special reason for you wanting to forget your troubles this evening?" Kate asked after Trish's sweeping declaration.

"None that I care to discuss," Trish mumbled dismissively. Instead of fussing with her hair or hurrying to repair her makeup, she simply propped her elbows on the narrow ledge of the vanity, rested her chin against the heels of her palms, and stared at her reflection in the mirror. "Men are royal pains in the neck," she said to no one in particular.

"I agree," Kate said, chuckling. "But a very necessary pain, don't you agree?"

"No," Trish said decisively as she squinted her eyes in order to focus on her friend. "They should all be loaded on a boat and sent somewhere."

"I'll see what I can do about it." Kate laughed. "Do you want me to stay with you or would you rather be alone?"

"I think I'd like to be alone. You can't imagine the relief it is not to have to listen to Josh's nephew talking nonstop and Damien snarling in my ear."

"Shall I relay that message to them?"

"You may."

After Kate had gone Trish drew a deep breath of relief and slowly exhaled. At last she was alone. Never before had she realized just how wonderful that feeling was. But even the hazy vagueness brought on by the margaritas couldn't dispel the reasoning behind her sudden yearning to closet herself away from the world. She was still rational enough in her thinking to know that the flimsy door to the lounge wasn't enough to keep Damien at bay.

After several more moments of thoughtful, but quite muddled, contemplation of her problems, she decided to return to the table. Perhaps she would sit by Nate, she thought maliciously as she rose to her feet. That way, she could keep Damien from doing bodily harm to Sean. Nate was a big boy; he was used to handling his darling brother.

The thought that she might possibly be able to annoy Damien in some small way brought a determined gleam to Trish's eyes as she made her way to the door. She stepped into the dimly lit hall that led to the dining room, thinking the evening might not be a total loss after all.

When a strong arm suddenly snaked around her waist from behind, Trish opened her mouth, ready to inform Damien that it was hardly necessary for him to stand guard outside the ladies' room. But before she could utter a single word, a large piece of cloth was jammed over her mouth and nose, and her head was jerked back against a hard chest and held immobile.

Trish tried to scream out, but her arms were pinned to her sides, and her feeble efforts to kick her assailant proved to be nothing more than wasted energy. She felt her body becoming limp, felt herself beginning to slip to the floor, an inexplicable lethargy creeping over her limbs. Even her eyelids seemed to be too heavy to keep open. A swirling blackness suddenly overtook her, unconsciousness wrapping her in its merciful folds.

CHAPTER ELEVEN

"I don't give a royal damn whether or not you ever catch the bastards!" Damien roared into the phone, his lips drawn back, his teeth clamped together like a steel trap. "I'm getting Trish the hell out of here. We've had two little visits from those creeps today, and that's about all I can stand."

"Use some common sense," Hal replied roughly. "Do you honestly think these attacks will stop if you take her someplace else? Be reasonable. They'll follow her to hell and back to get what they're after."

"Let 'em," Damien snarled. "I'll feel a hell of a lot safer on my own turf than harrowing around this damn place. It's all well and good to sit there and tell me to wait, Hal, but you haven't seen her. She's still out like a light. And speaking of that, my friend, just where the hell were your men? I can understand them not seeing whoever it was that left the note at the dog show, but that fiasco at the restaurant is stretching it a bit far."

"I'm sorry as hell, Damien, you know that. The only thing we can come up with is that the man had to have slipped through the kitchen. I had two good men right there in the dining room, and two outside the entire time your party was at the restaurant."

"I don't like it, Hal," Damien answered in a steely voice that was far more indicative of his real feelings than his ranting and raving. "Come up with some answers before I blow your investigation to hell and back."

"Give me a minute to think." Hal sighed. "Why don't I drop by later and have a chat with Trish?"

"Great!" Damien exploded. "That's all I need at this point. Not only will I have a patient on my hands but one refusing to speak to me."

"Then don't be a blabbermouth," Hal said curtly. "Let her assume you called on me for help. I don't think we'll accomplish anything by letting her know that at one time she was our prime suspect."

"Thanks for small favors," Damien replied sarcastically. "You'd better give us a couple of hours before you come over. The doctor told me that damn chloroform won't wear off for a while yet."

After his conversation with Hal, Damien

slammed down the receiver and bolted. He practically ran down the corridor to the room where Nate was watching over Trish.

"Is she awake yet?" he asked as soon as he stepped inside and closed the door, his deep blue gaze searching Trish's pale face.

"Not yet," Nate said quietly, alert to the near panic that still held Damien in its grip. "But she's been snoring like a foghorn. I wouldn't worry too much, she's only been out a little over an hour."

The rigid set of Damien's shoulders gradually relaxed as he heard this, and a slight flicker of a smile softened the forbidding line of his lips. "I know, and the doctor assured me she was in no danger from the chloroform or that bruise on her head. But I was worried just the same. Her snoring means she's relaxed."

"Margaritas, chloroform, and all." Nate laughed softly.

Damien grinned. "She adamantly denies doing such a terrible thing and will probably punch your lights out if you ever bring up the subject." He walked over to the bed and stared down at Trish, then bent and brushed his lips against her forehead, his hand smoothing her hair off her face.

Nate, an unwitting witness to the tenderness revealed in his brother's face, felt quite the interloper. Damien had always been his idol, seemingly indestructible as he'd taken on the responsibility of raising Nate and Barb after the accidental death of their parents. Damien was a fighter, a winner. He'd never lost at anything, until Trish. It had come close to destroying him, and the months following had been miserable for everyone connected with him.

Hopefully out of this experience would come a second chance for them, Nate thought as he watched the incredible tenderness sweep over Damien's hard face. If it didn't . . . He slowly shook his head, not wanting even to consider such a bleak happening.

He stepped forward and dropped a hand on Damien's shoulder. "I'm leaving now. I'll be in my room if you need me. Okay?"

"Thanks, Nate. Hopefully they won't try anything else for a while. If they follow their usual pattern, that is," Damien said with a bitter twinge to his voice. He turned back to stare at the sleeping Trish, Nate's leaving promptly fading from his mind as he watched her.

He'd never felt so helpless in his entire life. His enemies were usually men he could see, but this was an entirely different ball game, he grimly admitted. One that claimed no rules, no common ground for compromise. The enemy was an unknown force of evil with far-reaching tentacles that maimed and destroyed anyone who got in their way.

Trish felt as though she were climbing a mountain as she battled her way through the nebulous cloud of fuzziness that was holding her prisoner. The simple act of opening her eyes proved to be a task she wasn't ready for.

The right side of her face felt very peculiar, she thought dizzily, and she tentatively raised her fingers to the spot. She winced as they came in contact with the tender area.

This slight movement brought a deeply muffled oath and the sound of rapid footsteps approaching her bed. "Trish? Can you hear me?"

Why on earth was Damien shouting? she wondered vaguely, her brows knitting in annoyance. "Of co-course I can hear you. You're shouting loud enough," she croaked. Her own voice sounded strange to her for some reason.

"Never mind the way I sound," she heard Damien say. "Open your eyes."

"No thank you," she said primly. "I don't think I care to do that." Instead of yammering about her eyes, why couldn't he do something about the bed? It was spinning around like a child's top.

But instead of complying with her unspoken wishes he slipped his arm beneath her shoulders, and she felt the faint whisper of Damien's breath against her cheek.

"Don't be a such a little coward, sweetheart. Do as I tell you and open your eyes," he requested again, this time a little more gently.

"Why don't you just leave me alone?" she asked crossly, and then opened one eye a fraction of an inch, only to immediately close it and groan.

"What happened?" Damien roared, his hands clutching her shoulders. "Couldn't you see anything?" he asked, his voice sounding most peculiar.

"No," Trish said weakly. "I saw two of you sitting on the side of my bed. I'm afraid if I open both my eyes I'll find four. Since I can't even handle one of you, what on earth would I do with four?" she asked as seriously as if discussing something of grave importance.

"If I promise to send the others away, will you look at me then?" an amused Damien softly asked. He couldn't help but think that the chloroform had worn off, but the effect of the margaritas was still very much in evidence.

"Promise?"

"They're already gone."

"Are you sure?" She waggled one drooping finger at him.

"Absolutely. But they were the nicer copies of me. You should have kept them." Again his arm slipped beneath her shoulder. He raised her up and plumped another pillow behind her head. "Now look at me."

She did as she was instructed, and a pair of slightly squinting green eyes stared bemusedly into his worried blue ones. "There's nothing different about your face." She smiled accusingly, her gaze slipping and stumbling over features she found to be very familiar and comforting to her. The only thing she still couldn't explain was the scar that faded into his hairline near his temple. She raised a hand and let the tips of her fingers gently follow the rough edge. "That's new. It adds a sinister touch to your face."

"I'm glad you approve," Damien meekly replied, struggling to control his laughter in spite of the nightmare surrounding them. "I got that and the one on my thigh from the same bull. I'll convey your appreciation to him the next time I see him."

"Thank you," Trish said, sighing. She continued to stare at him, as if really seeing him for the first time in years. Her hand was resting on his shoulder, and she slowly began to knead the taut muscles beneath her fingers. "You feel tense."

A peculiar noise came rippling from the back of Damien's throat as he grabbed her hand and held it, his face turning quite pale . . . or so Trish thought as she watched him.

"Can you remember anything that happened at the restaurant?" he asked hoarsely, his breath rushing in and out in rapid gasps.

"Do you remember being attacked in the hallway just outside the ladies' lounge?"

"Unfortunately yes," Trish roughly sighed. "But I'd much rather talk about something else," she said querulously. "I can't imagine why that horrid person did such a thing to me. He stuck an awful rag in my face. It was filthy, I'm sure of it."

Damien sat and looked at her, an expression of complete frustration on his face. "It was the same bunch of bastards that have been following you for months, sweetheart," he tried again. "Only this time there was a witness. One of the busboys happened on the scene, and not only did he frighten the guy away, but he saw the character and was able to give the authorities a description. I also got in touch with Hal Langdon. Remember him? He'll be coming around later to ask you some questions."

"Really?" Trish smiled, then raised her arms above her head and stretched lazily, her mouth opening in a huge yawn. Damien's blue gaze followed the sudden thrusting of her breasts against the soft material of her gown and the arching of her narrow hips beneath the sheet. He felt like a starving man eyeing a morsel of food.

"Can we put his little talk off till later? I can think of other more enjoyable things to do than tell Hal about my accident. I'll let the busboy do that." She smiled, then reached out and slipped her fingers inside the opening of his shirt, almost sending Damien's senses reeling out of control. "This, for instance. I much prefer touching you than talking with your friends any old day."

"You need some coffee." Damien shot up from the bed as if he'd been burned. He reached for the phone and began dialing furiously. After curtly ordering coffee and sandwiches he dropped the receiver back onto the cradle and rubbed his neck, his eyes staring straight at the wall in front of him. "I'm sure once you've eaten something and have had some black coffee, you'll feel like talking. You hardly tasted your steak at dinner."

Trish threw back the sheet and pushed herself into a sitting position, a gleam of devilment in her eyes. But the sudden movement made the room spin wildly, and she clutched at the mattress for support. "Ohhhh," she gasped. "The whole room is spinning."

"I'm afraid nothing is going to help until those margaritas wear off," Damien reminded her defeatedly as he turned. He froze! He clenched his fists as he saw one strap of her gown slipping down, till one perfect, creamy breast shone before him. The pink nipple seemed like a tiny jewel beckoning to him.

He closed his eyes and inhaled deeply. His

lungs felt ready to burst as he tried to control the desire raging within him. He wanted Trish . . . God how he wanted her. But not in her present condition, not when her passion was the direct result of her having too much to drink.

He turned and made his way drunkenly toward the door, gulping in great breaths of fresh air as he stepped outside and slumped against the warm brick wall of the building. He had to be the biggest damn fool in the world, he thought disgustedly as he fought for control. But in his heart he knew that one night of making love to Trish wasn't enough. He wanted a lifetime with her.

When the pain of desire had slowly subsided, he turned and entered the room. He walked determinedly to the phone, called Hal, and put the meeting off till morning. Next he turned to the bed and the now sleeping Trish. With iron control stiffening his movements he eased the errant strap back into place. Then he removed the second pillow and pulled the sheet up and tucked it beneath her chin.

It was several hours later, after a very long, very cold shower and after having eaten all the sandwiches he'd ordered, that Damien went to bed. He dropped off to sleep with a tiny grin tugging at his lips, brought on by the steady, but gentle, snoring coming from the other bed.

Trish was certain she was being tortured by some horrible person. She had to be, she decided grimly as she tried to move her throbbing head and ended up gasping with pain. Dear Lord! What had caused her to feel like this? she wondered over and over again until finally the events of the evening paraded through her mind like some well-researched documentary. After several moments of embarrassing contemplation she sighed. She absolutely had to brush her teeth, she thought, and she never again wanted to see or hear the word *margarita!* There was also some niggling reminder of chloroform and somebody holding her very tightly, but she couldn't quite put her finger on what had happened.

With slow, painstaking movements she inched her way toward the edge of the bed and let her legs slide over the side. It took a superhuman effort to push herself into a sitting position, and that simple exertion left her biting her lips in an effort not to cry out against the pain it caused her.

Her weary gaze traveled over the early-morning darkness of the room till it reached the sprawled figure of Damien, asleep on the other bed. As her eyes adjusted to the narrow sliver of light showing from beneath the bathroom door, her lips curved into an unwittingly tender smile. She could see the tangled, rumpled mess he'd made of the covers. She could also see he was as naked as the day he was born. Trish wondered vaguely what it would take to get Damien into a pair of pajamas.

It wasn't until she was on her feet, silently groping her way to the bathroom, that she became aware of just what it was she was wearing and also that she had on nothing underneath it. So what? she argued with herself as she closed her eyes against the harsh light in the bathroom. She certainly hadn't been in any condition to undress herself. Would she somehow feel any less embarrassment if Damien had left her in her clothes? It certainly wasn't the first time he'd seen her body, she realized. Then she fleetingly thought, It probably won't be the last. She could hardly blame him for her silly attempt to become Miss Margarita of the Year.

Suddenly Trish realized she couldn't remember what had taken place on their return to the motel. Surely she hadn't entertained Damien with some sexy dance—had she? Or even worse, had she tried to seduce him?

With her fruitful imagination running full tilt, she strongly considered slipping from the room and disappearing from the face of the earth. That idea was infinitely more appealing than having to hear a recital of her evening's performance from Damien.

It wasn't until she felt brave enough to stare at her reflection in the mirror and in particular at the red spot on her temple that another scene from the previous evening came back to her. Not clearly, but enough for her to remember being attacked, and the fact that she'd felt pain in her head as she slipped to the floor.

Despite the discomfort she was feeling, Trish quickly set about unearthing her toothbrush. Remembering the attack had brought an alertness to her, an inquisitiveness as well as a ripple of fear that couldn't be put on hold till morning. She would awaken Damien and make him tell her everything that had happened. The pain in her head was forgotten as it dawned on her that her "friends" had seen fit to "communicate" twice with her in the same day.

CHAPTER TWELVE

It wasn't until she was halfway to the bed where Damien lay sleeping that Trish remembered he wasn't wearing a stitch. She came to an abrupt halt. She could go back to bed and wait until he awoke, she thought, and then immediately decided against it. If she called to him he was sure to jump to his feet, thinking she was in pain, and rush to her. That left only one alternative, she told herself. She would simply have to walk over to the bed, cover him with the sheet, then wake him up.

Armed with an idea she considered brilliant, she crept to the side of the bed and reached out to put thought into action. But instead of coming up with a handful of sheet to drape over Damien's thighs, Trish found her wrist caught in a tight grip. Before she could blink an eye, she was lying on her back. The edge of her gown was somewhere around her midriff, and Damien was propped on one elbow beside her.

"Have you added sleepwalking to your other unusual habits?" he demanded as he released her wrist. The callus-roughened palm of his hand started making slow, circular motions against the flat smoothness of her stomach, then began running fiery-hot over her quivering body from her thighs to the silken tips of her breasts. "How is your head?"

"Tender," she gulped as her heart leaped traitorously. Her head had suddenly become the least of her problems. "I need to talk to you," she said with all the determination she could muster. She tried to squirm free with arms and legs that had gone limp from memories of another time and place.

"I need to make love to you," he replied without hesitation and with far deeper conviction. With one clean sweep of his hand, he whisked the gown over her head and dropped it to the floor. Though the dimness of the room kept Trish from seeing the glowing intensity in Damien's eyes when he raised his head and stared at her, nothing could disguise the tone of his voice.

"Don't be ridiculous."

"I've never been more serious in my life, sweetheart."

"This isn't what I had in mind when I came over here," she whispered as his hand dipped lower to clasp the silken flesh of her inner thigh.

"It's what I've had in my mind since I looked across the lobby three days ago and saw you. Longer than that, even. I've had it in my mind since that bleak wintry day three years ago when you left me."

"Don't cloud the issue," Trish groaned as she struggled to overcome the spiraling flood of desire gathering within her. She gritted her teeth against the explosions going off in rapid succession in the pit of her stomach. She tried to ignore the unbelievably sensitive tips of his fingers as they touched and soothed her. "My life is in danger," she grasped feebly at the first thought that entered her mind. "I—I have to protect myself."

Damien began to kiss and nibble his way down her body, making exciting little forays against achingly familiar points of arousal before pausing, teasingly, over the center of her very being. When she felt the touch of his lips against her, a surge of need pulsed through her body with such force, she wasn't sure she would survive the onslaught.

"I'll protect you, my green-eyed witch," Damien moaned against the softness of her skin. "Just put everything else out of your mind and let yourself go."

"I'm so afraid, Damien." There were tears in her eyes. Tears of exquisite happiness at the completeness he was creating in her, but there were also tears for all the tomorrows to follow when that completeness would be replaced by an incredible emptiness that even time might not dispel.

"Fly with me, Trish darling, and let me calm your fears. It's been so lonely without you." He slowly, lovingly worked his way back up her body. When he was above her, supporting the weight of his upper body on his elbows, he stared like a drowning man into her eyes. "Part of me died when you walked out on me." He threw the accusation at her in a thick voice. "Have you ever seen a half-dead man stumbling aimlessly through life, Trish?"

She placed a finger against his lips. "Don't," she whispered, a rush of pity for him welling up in her, leaving an aching spot in her soul. His words had caught at her, bringing into focus the realization that he'd suffered as much as she. But her heart was divided, one part admitting this sobering fact, the other clutching the wounds of the past and refusing to let go.

Damien lowered his head and nibbled at the trembling fullness of her lips. "Mmmm. Your mouth tastes like peppermint."

"Toothpaste," Trish whispered, a tremulous smile curving her lips. She felt the pressure of his knee against hers and opened herself to him. With a rush of need that he couldn't control Damien entered her.

Trish cried out from the sheer beauty of the

sensations that were coursing through her body and she pushed hard against him, as if seeking to become part of him, to absorb him. Her hands gripped him closer, then released that grip to run feverishly up and down his back. She writhed beneath him, glorying in the exquisite feel of his skin against hers, of her nipples buried within the dark hair covering his chest.

When his mouth found its way to hers and his tongue forced its way between her lips, she welcomed it. She darted and teased and nipped at his lips in an uncontrollable urgency, stronger than any she'd ever known.

They were bound to each other by longing, by a deep-seated need that had exploded and was engulfing them in an inferno of passion unknown to either of them till now.

Damien's powerful thrusts increased in response to Trish's coaxing until their desire finally flung them helplessly into a world they'd known before. Their sharp cries of release came simultaneously, then a mindless, breathless moment consumed them and numbed their senses.

"I never dreamed it could actually be better than before, but it was," Damien murmured gently against Trish's hair moments later.

"Neither did I," she whispered, still awed by the depth of emotion she had felt. She didn't want to think of that emotion as love. She'd gotten over that long ago, or so she kept repeating to herself. But there was something. Something elusive and mysterious that kept worrying her. She tried to move, but Damien's arms tightened.

"Feeling threatened?" he rasped.

"I'm terrified" was her honest answer. "It took me years to get over you. I could never go through that again."

"Hmmm. I'm not sure I like hearing myself described as something that has to be gotten over. Nor do I like hearing that you were successful. But there's really no sense in arguing the point, is there?" He turned so that he was on his side and could see her face. "We both know you're lying."

"You still go for the throat, don't you?" Trish frowned as one hand idly traced the outline of his ear.

"Where you are concerned, yes," he said bluntly. "I want you back. There's no other way of putting it." His hand at her waist tightened. "I want to be married to you again—I want you to have my baby. I want the same things I wanted five years ago."

"Babies." She shuddered. "You never give up, do you? Why can't you accept the fact that I'm not cut out to be a mother? I certainly have."

"Because I don't believe such a ridiculous

thing," he said harshly. "I know the kindness that's in you, Trish. There's a wealth of gentleness inside you. I also remember seeing that look of tenderness that would come over your face when you used to hold our friends' children, remember?" He gave a rough sigh, his big hand caressing and kneading her flat stomach. "It's not that you don't want babies, honey, there's something else eating at you. I only wish I knew what it was."

"This conversation reminds me of the last year of our marriage, Damien," she muttered stubbornly. "You were constantly going on about me becoming pregnant. Well, haven't you been keeping up with things? There's no reason in the world why you can't have a baby. You can adopt one."

"And that's a wonderful thing for couples without hope, isn't it?" he surprised her by saying. "But that isn't our problem, is it, honey? No," he calmly continued, "I'll wait. You may be a bit slow and stubborn, but in time you'll see it my way."

Trish suddenly felt a wave of resentment sweeping over her. "What I 'see' is a stubborn, narrow-minded jerk who refuses to accept any other point of view but his own. I—"

Her furious rush of words was interrupted by Damien's mouth swooping down and capturing hers in a kiss that sent the blood rushing to her head and had her clutching his shoulders as tiny fingers of desire caught her in their grip.

"You're not fighting fair!" Trish gulped a mouthful of air as she struggled free. "I'll be damned if I'll let you charm me into agreeing to God knows what, with your slick words and your deft hands and your . . ."

"Yes, darling?" Damien chuckled. "My what?"

"Don't 'darling' me, you conceited fool! I know exactly what you're up to. I lived with you for two years, and I can tell what you're thinking even before you say it."

"I know, sweetheart," he consoled her, his breath ruffling her hair as his tongue teased her earlobe. His fingers traced delicate patterns against the sensitive skin of her inner thighs. Then he clasped his hand tight against that part of her that was the core of her femininity.

"It won't work, Damien," she said in a strangled voice, gritting her teeth against the swirling fire he was igniting within her. "I'm stronger than you."

"Of course you are, darling," he breathed softly, his lips feathering their way down to close about one small, swollen nipple. "You're a tower of strength," he murmured against her breast.

"I'll make you pay for this, Damien," she said, trying to sound angry, but her voice

161

came out like a moan. Her hands blatantly disobeyed the rigid dictates of her mind by burying themselves in the thick dark hair on his head and pressing him closer to her.

"I know, and I can hardly wait for the fight to begin. You're always such a generous loser, sweetheart."

Trish gave up then. Damien had always been an expert at manipulating her emotions, and he had once again met with success. Her body was purring, curving to meet the wave of passion that would soon envelop yet another explosion of climactic splendor.

"After what Damien told me when we talked last night, and after listening to your story this morning, Trish, I've spent most of my time on the telephone," Hal Langdon said to her. "Unfortunately," he continued, his expression sobering, "I'm afraid you won't be too happy with what I found out."

Trish threw Damien a questioning glance, then turned her attention back to Hal. It was early afternoon, and the three of them were seated around the small table in the motel room. Trish had felt a tremendous surge of relief when she learned that Damien had enlisted his old friend's help. But after recalling that Hal had gone with the Drug Enforcement Agency some years earlier, she wondered how he could possibly help her, and said as much to Damien.

"Different agencies do work together on occasions, honey," he'd told her. "Don't worry, Hal will know what to do. And from what you've told me, the local authorities you've been dealing with certainly haven't been very cooperative."

Trish had agreed. She'd gotten to know Hal when she was married to Damien, and was fond of him. She'd also reached the point where any help would be welcomed if it would allow her to get on with her life and forget the trauma she'd lived through for the past three months.

"Exactly what have you come up with?" she asked.

"Are you aware of the drug smuggling on Shoppal Island?" Hal asked.

"Drug smuggling!" Trish exclaimed. She gave Hal a rueful grin. "As much as I'd like for you to be able to clear up this mystery, I honestly think you're letting your imagination run away with you. Shoppal is the last place I'd think of as a smuggler's mecca. It's so quiet and peaceful."

Hal shifted uncomfortably in his chair, his fingers fidgeting with a book of matches he picked up from the table. "I hate to disagree with you, honey, but we have information that leads us to believe that it has become just

163

that." He quoted an estimated amount of money made yearly from the drug smuggling operations on the island, and Trish gasped.

"That's incredible," she murmured, then frowned. She disliked hearing such a story about the place where she'd grown up, but at the moment, *her* problems were her immediate concern. "I'm sure this is a silly question, but why are you telling me about this?"

Hal shot Damien a cautious look and then, after a brief pause, he continued. "We have reason to suspect that your father was involved in smuggling drugs onto the island whenever he returned from a dog show."

For several long seconds Trish simply stared at him. "Then I hope you'll forgive me if I consider you and your agency to be a group of fools," she said sharply. "Did you happen to speak to a Sergeant Decker during all that time you spent on the phone this morning?"

"Yes, I did," Hal said, nodding. "Why?"

"Because he began hinting that my father was involved in something from almost the first moment after he arrived at the scene of the crime. He and I have had several arguments regarding the subject. In fact"—she pinned the lanky investigator with a scathing look—"I threatened to have him thrown out the last time he came to my shop. Did he tell you about that?" she demanded.

"No." Hal looked about as miserable as a man possibly could. "He didn't mention that. But I'm afraid his assumptions have some merit, honey."

"If you believe that," she said, her green eyes stormy, "then I really don't think I care to talk to you." She started to push back her chair and rise, but Damien stopped her.

"Hear him out, Trish." His quiet voice of authority and his firm hold on her hand stopped her.

A stubborn expression swept over Trish's face as she looked at each of the men seated at the table. "My father was not involved in drug smuggling," she stated quietly and firmly. "It's not very pleasant having to sit and listen to a bunch of wild accusations regarding his character."

"There are no accusations here, Trish, only suspicions," Hal corrected her. "There's a world of difference."

"Not nearly enough when someone you love is the one suspected of a crime. There are people who judge, convict, and sentence a person on a few words of gossip carelessly spoken. And believe me, Sergeant Decker's accusations have been about as harmless as a rattlesnake. I never dreamed he hated my father so much."

"What about Michael Tolar?" Hal asked.

"What about him?" Trish asked.

"How did he come to work for your father?"

"I believe he was with another handler in California before coming to my father. He was hired while I was . . . in Texas. Why?" she asked. "Is he a suspect as well?"

"His name's been mentioned," Hal said, dodging a direct answer.

"Doesn't it strike you as odd that the two prime targets of all these wild accusations are both dead?" Trish was hurt, angry, and humiliated. From the moment Damien had told her that Hal was going to help her, she'd felt as though a great weight had been lifted from her shoulders. But instead of helping, he seemed intent on compounding her problem. She found herself in the distasteful position of being forced to cooperate with him or run the risk of never clearing her father's name.

"Odd, indeed," Hal agreed. "However, we know Tolar's death was an accident. Your father's death remains a mystery. If—and please note that I said *if*—he was the main means of transporting the dope, then why was he killed? It's a question we've been trying to figure out for months."

"Perhaps it really was an accident," Damien spoke up. He turned to Trish. "Didn't you say that at one time Sergeant Decker suggested that John could have surprised some burglars as they tried to rob the kennel?"

"Yes," she said, slowly nodding, "he did. And there were a rash of burglaries on the island during that same time. Unfortunately he rather quickly changed his mind when I, along with several of the local residents, began pressing him for some sort of progress in the case."

"I'd like to go back to a question you asked me earlier, Trish, about how all this ties in with what's been happening to you," Hal remarked. He leaned forward and placed his forearms on the edge of the table, a slight frown wrinkling his forehead. "Damien tells me that in all your communications with the person or persons unknown who have been threatening you, the one thing they keep demanding is that you give them their property. Do you have any idea what they could be talking about?"

"No," she firmly answered. "And I sincerely hope you aren't thinking that I'm hiding a stash of drugs somewhere." She glared at him. "Is that what all this is really about? Do you think I took over when my father died?"

"Not at all," Hal lied so convincingly and so smoothly, Damien was tempted to reach out and hug him. "We realize that the harassment you've been receiving is being done out of desperation, hoping to frighten you into handing over what we assume to be a shipment of cocaine."

"My God!" Trish turned pale. "I thought you were talking about a pound or two of marijuana. I never dreamed we were discussing cocaine." She turned a dazed face to Damien. "That's serious," she gasped.

"Precisely." Hal nodded. "Once I learned from you and Damien what had been going on, I couldn't tell you how relieved I was that he decided to buy another bull."

Trish missed the quick look that passed between the two men, still shocked by what she'd been told. Cocaine, she thought dazedly, those idiots think I have their shipment of cocaine! Then just as quickly her shock turned to fear as the memory of her father's death flashed through her mind. Oh, Dad, she silently cried, you couldn't have, you simply couldn't have.

"Wouldn't it be simpler for you and your department to offer me some sort of protection?" She posed the question in a shaky voice without looking at Damien. "I mean—Damien does have responsibilities at home, and if I continue as planned, I'll be in Florida for at least another three days."

CHAPTER THIRTEEN

Trish was still sitting in the chair at the table staring fixedly into space. Just outside the door to the motel room she could hear the low murmur of voices as Hal and Damien talked. But even if they had been shouting she wouldn't have heard them.

Emotionally she was a wreck. Not only had she just found out about the suspicions the authorities had about her father, but she had just been informed by Hal that, due to the rather unusual circumstances surrounding her particular case, he couldn't give her blanket protection. He had said that Damien would have to continue doing that.

"But why not?" she all but yelled at him. "I'm a taxpayer, and I'm also a hell of a nice person when I'm not being chased by a bunch of crazies." How could she tell him that she'd rather be closeted for days with a complete stranger than have to spend another minute alone with Damien? She would have sounded like a nut telling Hal that she was in almost as much fear of having her heart broken as she was of being physically harmed. And that would surely happen if Damien stayed.

"I can't help you," Hal had said, "because it's imperative that they not know my agency is involved. If you suddenly appear with an army of bodyguards surrounding you there's no telling how long it would take to clear up this mess. Do you understand?" he asked softly.

Three more days. She closed her eyes against the immediate future, seeing in her mind the unbelievable strain she would be under if she did as Hal suggested. He had no way of knowing what it was he was asking. He had no way of knowing that if she stayed with Damien it would quite likely destroy her.

But what other choice did she have? she asked herself. Perhaps she could talk with Damien, in hopes of appealing to that gentle streak she knew existed beneath his tough exterior. It was worth a try, she decided; it was definitely worth a try.

Twenty minutes later Trish realized how foolish she'd been to think Damien had a gentle bone in his obnoxious body.

"That's the craziest suggestion I've ever heard!" she exclaimed. With jerky movements she stubbed out the cigarette she'd just

170

lit and sprang to her feet, unable to believe she had heard Damien right.

"It's the only sensible solution, considering what Hal just told me," Damien replied as he lay on the bed, his back and shoulders leaning against the padded headboard. He didn't appear to have heard her less than kind remark, or, if he had, he chose to ignore it.

"What did your friend Hal say that would prompt you to do something as ridiculous as asking me to marry you?" Trish demanded. She began pacing the narrow path from the door to the dressing room, privately consigning both Hal and Damien to hell.

"He simply asked me to try to prepare you for the fact that there's little hope of solving this case within three days. Then he told me he didn't think you'd be in any real danger back home as long as someone stayed with you—someone like me, for instance. If the men following you learn that I'm there permanently, as your husband, they might start acting differently."

"Why didn't he tell *me?*" Trish snapped, never breaking stride. "Did he suddenly become mute?"

"Really, Trish," Damien said, "I don't recall you being so emotional when we were married. You should watch that. Continual emotional outbursts create stress, and stress

171

causes lines in your face," he smugly informed her.

She swung around and faced him. "You may take your stress, your lines, *and* your marriage proposal and go straight to hell!"

Damien cocked one heavy brow and grinned. "You've wounded me. I've offered you my heart, my name, and half my fortune, only to have you turn me down. How can you be so cruel?"

"How can *you* be so ridiculous?" she snapped back at him. "How can you have the nerve to even consider asking me to marry you again when there's no reason in the world for me to do so?"

Trish tried desperately to call on all the old hurts to reinforce her resentment toward Damien. But it took only seconds for her to realize it wouldn't work. In spite of the fear that was stalking her, she saw desire in his eyes and felt a warm rush of color steal over her face as she remembered the night before and how easily she'd fallen into his arms. As much as she wanted to throw all the blame on Damien, she knew it wasn't possible. She'd done everything but beg him to make love to her.

As she looked at Damien reclining on the bed, Trish realized she had also seen something else in his eyes, a look of uncertainty, almost desperation. It had only been there an instant when he had spoken of their remarriage, and it completely belied his relaxed appearance and self-assured words. Trish couldn't help but feel a little sorry for this man who was willing to grasp at any straw to make her his wife again. He did love her, she admitted to herself. Too bad what they had had together was so completely over.

"Let me help you, Trish," Damien said softly. He swung his feet to the floor, then reached toward her with one hand. "Come here—please."

She could once again see his need for her, a need that went far beyond the physical, and slowly, resignedly, she moved forward, ignoring the warning signals sounding in her head. When she was within easy reach of Damien, she let her hand slip into his and allowed him to draw her down onto his lap.

"Marry me, Trish." His voice was husky, his hands gentle as they framed her face. "I've never stopped loving you, and after last night, I don't think you have the nerve to say you've stopped caring for me."

"No, I haven't stopped caring, Damien," she said, sighing. "But caring for someone is supposed to bring happiness, contentment, fulfillment." She shook her head, a sad smile pulling at her lips. "Neither of those things held a place of honor in our marriage for very long, did they?"

A rush of annoyance swept over Damien's features at this remark. "There's no need to relive each disagreement we had. Why can't you put the past behind you and let us get on with the future, a future together."

"Because the past has an uncanny way of spoiling the future," she said softly, trying to reason with him. "We had problems, Damien, problems that still exist. We'd be the biggest fools in the world to rush into another marriage just because you feel you must protect me. Besides, we don't have to be married first for you to spend a little time at my house. I'm sure our marital status isn't of overwhelming concern to the men who are following me," she chided gently.

Instead of arguing, Damien caught her chin in one hand and slipped his other arm around her. The moment his mouth took possession of hers, Trish felt herself melting into him. She knew she could offer all sorts of arguments about why they shouldn't kiss, why they shouldn't make love, even why they shouldn't be together, but the moment she felt his arms around her, the reasons seemed unimportant.

She caressed the broad thickness of his shoulders, loving the familiar feel of him beneath her touch. The desire he awakened so easily within her began to heighten her awareness of his scent, of the crispness of his thick, dark hair, and of the texture of his skin. She could feel the fire of his own passion swirl around her, as it had done in the past, licking and nipping and claiming her with an overwhelming assurance Trish had never understood.

With the motions of a man drugged Damien slowly raised his head, his eyes smoldering with passion. "What argument can you raise now, Trish, that would make me believe you don't love me, mmmm?" He cupped one tender breast in the palm of his hand, his thumb finding its excited tip and slowly brushing against it. "Your body is alive, warm, and responsive to my touch. Your heart is racing like crazy. Why can't you accept the inevitable and stop fighting me?"

"Because it takes more than good sex to make a marriage work." She slowly let out the breath she'd been holding, quietly comparing his single-mindedness to the dull throbbing of an aching tooth. "There are so many things we don't agree on. Shall I refresh your memory by naming seven or eight of them?" It was so comfortable in his arms, she thought regretfully, why couldn't he be content with what they had at the moment and not try to arrange their future?

"If you mean your career, don't worry. We can work around that."

Trish drew back and stared suspiciously at him. "Oh? Just what do you have in mind?"

"Move your business to Texas," he surprised her by saying. "Hire some competent help. Then, when you get pregnant, you won't be worried when you have to leave."

"When will you get it through your thick head that I have no desire to juggle my career around two-A.M. feedings and the patter of little feet?" she lashed out. Without another word she slipped off his lap, feeling like a first-class fool for having been there in the first place.

Damien rose to his formidable height, his narrowed gaze skipping over her face and lingering over the fullness of her lips. "Haven't you learned not to make rash statements, Trish? Before the year is up you'll be my wife, and I hope you'll be carrying my baby. If that puts a crimp in your career, then so be it." He turned and walked toward the door but paused when his hand grasped the knob. "There's another reason I think you should consider my proposal of marriage."

"Oh, I'm sure there are several," Trish snapped. "What is this one?"

"Your enemies have gone to great lengths to smear your father's reputation, and they're going to do the same thing to you. They've already set the stage by making sure there was nobody around when they called you. I'm

176

sure you learned, when you complained to Sergeant Decker, just what he thought of such charges. In his eyes you already were a somewhat hysterical young woman. Besides, Hal thinks our getting married would be an excellent idea." He continued to regard her for several seconds, then said, "Remember, we're supposed to have dinner with Kate and Josh."

After he'd gone Trish sank to the edge of the bed, her thoughts in a turmoil. As badly as she hated to admit it, she knew he had a point. Sergeant Decker had tried from the beginning to make her look as ridiculous as possible. Each complaint she'd lodged with him had been quickly dismissed, bringing an outburst from Trish. He probably did have her pegged as an overemotional woman. At least Hal hadn't appeared to feel that way, she thought.

She couldn't help but wonder what else Hal had suggested to Damien. Was their lovemaking somehow part of the plan to protect her? But the moment the question came to mind, Trish dismissed it. She knew Damien too well not to recognize genuine desire and passion in him. Perhaps the proposal of marriage had been Hal's idea. Regardless, though, she told herself, she couldn't go through with such a sham.

But are you willing to risk doing anything

that will perpetuate the awful suspicions that threaten to destroy your father's good name? she asked herself. Does it have to be marriage to Damien? she silently argued. Trish was well aware of his stubbornness. When he went after something, he fought a no-holds-barred battle. A brittle gleam of suspicion edged its way into the green depths of her eyes as she tried to come to some decision. Damien had said he wanted her back as his wife. But why? Trish knew in her heart that until she felt there was a chance for their marriage to work, she would never accept his proposal. She couldn't possibly settle for less.

"Am I to assume from that dark scowl hovering over your ugly puss that Trish wasn't exactly enamored with the idea of keeping you on as her roommate?" Hal asked innocently, his lips quirking at the dirty look Damien threw him.

"I don't remember you looking so great a little while ago when you were stumbling and fumbling your way through lie after lie," Damien snapped. "Why didn't you tell her that at one time you thought she was smuggling dope?"

"Because I didn't relish the thought of having a hatchet buried between my ears," he said quite honestly. "You do realize that the chances of us clearing up this little matter in three days are almost nonexistent, don't you?" Hal asked on a more serious note.

"Of course. I've made arrangements to go back to Shoppal with her. Nate will be joining us as well. Supposedly Charlie will be heading back to Texas in the morning with a bull I bought from Josh."

Hal grinned. "Have you *told* her that you and Nate will be traveling back to Shoppal with her?"

"I'll tell her later."

After thumbing through a ragged note pad, Hal said, "Under no circumstances is she to change her schedule. I want her to make the last three shows and act as though nothing at all is bothering her. I've called in some extra agents, and we'll be watching every move the two of you make. In fact"—he looked over at Damien, his homely face dead serious—"I wouldn't even let her go to the bathroom alone."

The look that passed between them left any further words regarding Trish's safety unnecessary. They'd been through bad situations together in the years past. And though it was the first time a loved one had been threatened, they each knew what they had to do.

"We'll be away for two or three hours this evening," Damien broke the easy silence that had drifted over them. "We're having dinner at Josh's place."

"We'll be watching," Hal assured him.

Going to Josh's home for dinner seemed the most normal thing in the world to Trish. For years he'd invited crowds of people out to his place after the dog show.

The house was as beautiful as Trish remembered. And even though it had been a number of years since her last visit, it was still as warm and comfortable as when she had last gone there with her father.

"I can't tell you what a scare that was last night," Kate began the minute she and Trish were alone in the kitchen. "Are you sure you're all right?"

"I'm fine," Trish said, smiling. "Although I'm not too sure I'll ever drink another margarita."

"Josh repeated to me a little of what Damien told him, enough for us to know that the last three months of your life have been pure hell."

Trish nodded. "But I'm sure it will all be over before long. The authorities are working on the case now, so I don't feel quite so desperate as I did." She gave her friend an apologetic smile. "I'm sorry, but I was warned not to discuss what's been happening with my friends. I do hope you understand, Kate. Apparently these idiots hounding me wouldn't hesitate to try to get information from anyone they thought I'd taken into my confidence."

"Don't worry." Kate threw up her hands in a gesture of understanding. "I may be as curious as a cat, but even I know when not to poke my nose into something. The only thing I want you to know is that I'm here if you need me."

"Thanks, Kate. I appreciate that."

And she really did, Trish thought later as she relaxed beside the pool and watched the dappled reflections of the moon dance across the gleaming surface. It was the first really pleasant evening she'd had in months. Everyone had left her alone, as if they knew she needed time to herself. They were seated nearby, but for all Trish heard of or participated in the conversation, she could have been thousands of miles away.

When she felt the touch of Damien's hand on hers and heard him tell her it was time to go, she felt nothing but regret.

"We'll take a nice long cruise when this mess is over," he told her several minutes later as they began to drive back to town. His hand found its way to her thigh, and Trish didn't bother moving away from his touch. She was aware that it carried no sexual overtones but just showed that he wanted to be physically connected with her in some way.

"Am I so easy to read?" She smiled at him. Even her smile was different, she thought as she let her gaze flow over him. Different in that during those quiet, soul-searching moments by the pool she'd come to the realization that she could never marry Damien again. It wouldn't work. She'd also accepted the fact that for as long as they were together she would sleep with him. She hadn't planned the time or the hour, but she knew it would happen as surely as the next breath she drew.

"You're taking a long time answering me," she said quietly. "Was my question that difficult?"

"Not difficult in the sense that I can't find an answer," Damien said, giving her a glowing look. "My difficulty is that I have to decide which answer will keep you with that lovely, relaxed look on your face. As for being easily read"—he inhaled deeply—"I know your moods and the way you think as well as I know my own self. Deep love does that for a person, don't you agree?"

"I refuse to answer on the grounds that I—"

Her lighthearted reply was hastily cut off by a string of curse words exploding from Damien's lips. "What's wrong?" she cried as she saw him jam his foot against the accelerator and found herself being jerked by the sudden speed of the car.

"Just stay calm, honey," he ground out between clenched teeth. "We've picked up your friends. Apparently they've been following with their lights out until we reached this section of the road."

"Why this particular section?" Trish asked, her voice shrill with alarm.

"It's dotted with curves, and there appears to be a ditch on either side of the road." He threw her a quick, reassuring glance, meant to erase some of the fear he saw etched in her face. "Try not to worry, sweetheart. We're not far from the city limits, and I doubt even those bastards back there are anxious to draw a crowd."

It occurred to Trish as she sat like a statue, her eyes darting from the rapidly rising speedometer to the dark shadows of the trees beside the highway, that they could crash. And if they did, at the rate of speed they were traveling they would probably be killed. Suddenly a peculiar calm settled over her. She turned her head toward Damien, the lights from the dash enabling her to see the film of perspiration on his forehead as he fought to keep the car on the road and at the same time keep the car behind them from running them off the road. If this was it, she told herself, then she was glad he was with her. Without thought or plan, the words "I love you" slipped from between her lips in a gentle whisper.

CHAPTER FOURTEEN

Trish reached for a towel and then stepped from the shower, her knees still weak from the wild ride. After a brisk rub her skin was a rosy pink underneath her light honey-tan. In the few minutes it took her to slip into a pink-and-white-striped nightshirt and run the brush through her hair, some of the tension had eased from her body. She gave one last look in the mirror, then opened the door.

As soon as she stepped from the bathroom, Trish could hear Damien talking. She walked on into the room, not even trying to hide the fact that she was listening to his conversation.

"I'll tell her, Hal," he said in a disapproving voice. "But if she doesn't want to go along with the idea, then I certainly won't force her."

There was a long pause, and Trish could see the tiny muscle throbbing in Damien's cheek. Evidently he and Hal were at cross purposes, she thought as she waited for the conversation to end.

"I'm not surprised, are you? A privately owned car can be traced. The one they were driving was probably stolen."

After another lengthy silence Damien's expression grew darker. He finally agreed to whatever it was Hal was saying to him and then slammed down the receiver.

"Are you and Hal disagreeing about something?" Trish asked. She walked over to the bed and sat down beside him.

Damien ran his hands over his face, then dropped them to his thighs, his face looking haggard. "He still insists we make the other three shows as originally planned." He looked at Trish, his expression softening. "Personally, I think it's a damn stupid idea. It's obvious these characters have decided to step up their attacks on you, and I don't like it. I think it would be far safer if we packed it up and headed back to Shoppal."

"Are you planning on going to Shoppal with me?" she asked, surprised, the question momentarily taking precedence over the immediate problem of her personal safety. She'd reconciled herself to three more days in Damien's company. Having him on the island for an indefinite period of time was more than she'd bargained for.

"Yes, and Nate as well. Can you think of a

better idea?" he asked curtly. "Without the protection of someone you can trust you'll be a sitting duck." There was a curious tension in his body as he waited for her answer.

Trish's first thought was to try to put him off with some tale of there being another man waiting for her, but common sense warned her that it would be wasted energy. Damien could read her like a book. "No," she honestly admitted.

"Then don't you think it would be somewhat silly for me to have stayed so close to you while you're here in Florida and then calmly wave good-bye and get in my car and return to Texas and leave you to face God knows what when you get home?"

She had to smile at his remarks. Damien was never one to leave things to chance. He'd made his decision to protect her, and come hell or high water, he would do just that.

"Naturally, when examined from that viewpoint, I can see why you would want to come with me." She grinned facetiously, then reached out and placed a hand on his arm. "I didn't mean to sound ungrateful, Damien. But being with you is something of a strain."

"Why?" he asked cautiously, his dark brows drawn together above his blue eyes.

"Because"—she looked him straight in the eye—"my being with you is comparable to an alcoholic finding himself locked in a distillery.

186

In short, my darling ex-husband, I'm finding myself becoming more and more embroiled in a situation as old as man. To put it bluntly, I'm beginning to have designs on your stubborn, pigheaded, domineering body. I don't think I have to tell you that I'm not pleased with this realization, do I?"

"To put it bluntly, my darling ex-wife," he mimicked, "I think you would welcome a motorcycle gang into your home before you'd welcome me. But at least your, shall we say, honest, confession gives me hope," he replied sourly.

Trish flopped back on the bed, her arms raised and her hands clasped behind her head. "Have you ever stopped to consider what an exciting life we're leading, Damien?" Her voice was tinged with sarcasm. "I'm being chased by a bunch of unknown thugs wanting to recover their blasted cocaine, and intent on inflicting pain or worse on my cowardly body, while you, who just *happened* to arrive in the midst of the conflict, now find yourself in the unpleasant role of my bodyguard. Isn't it wonderful how fate has thrown the two of us back together again? Why, I can hardly believe my good fortune."

Damien leaned back on the bed, his upper body braced by an elbow as he stared at her, amusement lurking in his eyes. "I'm sure you thank your lucky stars at least ten times a day."

"Oh, at least," she quickly agreed, then lapsed into thoughtful silence during which Damien made no effort to touch her.

This was a different Trish, he decided as he watched the way the feathery tips of her lashes made tiny shadows against her skin. He could handle an angry Trish, even an emotional one. But one who admitted wanting him in a voice as flinty as steel was a new experience. He felt remarkably like a bomb expert. If he touched the wrong wire the bomb would explode and he would be destroyed.

"I absolutely refuse to marry you again, you know."

Damien blinked at the suddenness of her statement. "I think you've gotten that message across," he quietly remarked. What the hell was wrong with her? he wondered.

"Aren't you going to argue with me? Tell me how ridiculous I'm being?" Trish demanded.

"No. I prefer to tear down your defenses by other means."

"Such as?"

"A wise man never divulges his secrets."

"But are you wise, Damien? Was it wise to interrupt your plans and become involved in my problems?"

188

"You *are* part of my plans, Trish," he told her in a quiet, steady voice. "I'll admit I haven't lain awake at night trying to figure out ways to get you back, but believe me, you've been in my thoughts more than anything else in my life."

Trish found herself unable to distinguish between the need for him that had lain dormant within her for so long and the feeling of desperation brought on by the terrifying events that had taken control of her life. The last thing she wanted to admit was that she needed Damien to make love to her. But she did, and nothing but his hands and his lips on her body could control the fire that was slowly growing within her.

She lay staring at him, her lips parted and her breathing quickening as her thoughts became more fully centered on the feel of his hard, strong body holding her prisoner.

With a boldness she'd never shown during their marriage Trish reached out and began to loosen the buttons of his shirt. As her fingers became dedicated to this task she heard the sharp intake of Damien's breath and saw his broad chest expand.

"What are you doing, honey?" he rasped in a tortured voice.

"I'm seducing you," she said slowly. She leaned forward and let the tip of her tongue touch his exposed chest.

189

"But we—"

"Don't talk," she whispered. "Just love me."

Damien reacted to that softly spoken plea without hesitation. He crushed her to him, his wide hands running feverishly over her body.

Their clothes were disposed of with a quickness that bespoke the urgency of the moment. Their hands became exquisite instruments through which pleasure, raw and wild, was administered to limbs quivering with desire.

Trish floated in a swirl of eroticism as Damien claimed each throbbing inch of her body with his lips and his touch. She tried to pull him up to her, but he resisted. "Not yet, princess," he murmured against the glowing softness of her thighs. "Not yet."

Heady showers of color exploded behind the dark wall of her closed eyes as he continued to tease and coerce a response from her. Tiny, convulsive spasms shuddered through her as his hands cupped the fullness of her breasts.

When finally he covered her thighs with his hard, hot ones, Trish groaned with desire. Her legs parted and became human bonds around him, binding him to her as she sought to entrap him in a world of breathless enchantment.

The moment she felt him enter her and

begin a deliberately slow and agonizing rhythm, something snapped within her, and she lost all sense of time and place. The gold of her hair became a continual shimmering mass as her head twisted from one side to the other on the pillow. Barely audible words of endearment found their way past her lips to Damien's ears.

Finally the moment of relief came as they both cried out, overcome with pleasure.

Long moments later, Trish reached up with one hand and pushed back a shock of hair that was tickling the side of her neck. Instead of moving away from the warm body that was at her side, she turned her face to Damien's. She touched her tongue to his lips and tasted the salty sheen left on his body from their love-making. She smiled in the darkness, the smell of him drugging her senses and leaving her with a sense of completeness.

The next three days were spent as Hal had ordered, with Trish, Nate, and Damien duly attending the dog shows.

"Have you ever considered making a house dog out of Jax?" Nate asked her on the morning of the first show. He was watching her ready the dogs for the ring and was clearly amused by the entire process.

"No." Trish laughed. "He's too undisciplined. Why?"

"Well," he confessed, "the last couple of

nights, since the dogs have been staying in my room, I let him out of his crate. You should have seen that rascal, Trish. He made a bee-line for the bed and plopped his head down on one of the pillows as if he knew exactly what it was for."

"Don't be taken in by him," she warned. "He's a complete rogue."

"No, you're not, are you, fella?" Nate crooned as he held Jax's head against his chest and carefully patted him on his neck. "Tell your mistress that you aren't nearly as silly as she and my jerk of a brother are."

"What's that crack supposed to mean?" Trish eyed him nastily.

"It means, my darling sister-in-law, that I've never seen two people who enjoy in-flicting pain on each other any more than you and Damien."

"Oh? And just who made you an authority on the subject?"

"I'm no expert, squirt, but the electricity that crackles between you two is enough to scorch anyone who gets in the way. Damn it, why can't you two get your act together and quit all this hell-raising? And besides that, I miss you."

The sharp retort that had sprung readily to her lips at the beginning of his lecture became a gentle smile as Trish met his embarrassed gaze. "I've missed you, too, Nate. And

192

Barb and Walt, and all the people I got to know while I lived in Texas."

"What about Damien? Have you missed him as well?" Nate asked gently.

"Him most of all. And seeing him again has created a strange mixture of emotions for me to deal with."

"Such as?"

"Such as a resurgence of the love I feel for him as well as remembering the way we tried to destroy each other. I really don't want to think about not seeing him again. So"—she shrugged—"I'm faced with a decision that, right or wrong, will affect the rest of my life."

CHAPTER FIFTEEN

"Gosh, it's good to be back home." Trish sighed as she scrambled into the car beside a frowning Damien. "Sorry I took so long, but Gordy has been talking nonstop ever since she got here this morning. I'm not sure bringing a former housekeeper out of retirement—especially the one that raised me—is such a good idea. I honestly expected her to grab me and check behind my ears."

"How the hell were you able to put up with that constant yammering?" Damien asked grouchily. "If she worked for me the first thing I'd do would be to place a two-inch strip of tape over her damn mouth."

"My, my," Trish said, grinning at him. "Aren't you Mr. Cheerful this morning. What's the matter, didn't you sleep well last night? Or is your buddy Hal being difficult again? Is he still trying to push you into marrying me?"

Damien shot her a look that had her cheeks

flaming. "He doesn't have to push, and you know it. As for my night, you know perfectly well how that went, Miss Priss, because you spent every minute with me. I'll admit I didn't get much sleep, but then—who wants to sleep when they can make love to a beautiful witch like you?"

"You're impossible." Trish tried to sound stern. She turned crimson cheeks to the window and stared out at the familiar landmarks that dotted the island. "Did you and Nate find anything when you searched the kennel?"

"Not unless the bastards harassing you plan to start handling dogs for a living. And don't try to change the conversation, Trish darling. I was merely reassuring you that my night was an unbelievable time of pure joy." Damien chuckled. She felt the weight of his hand as he placed it on her shoulder. "Does it embarrass you for me to tell you that you are one hell of a sexy lady?"

"Certainly not—yes." Trish floundered, not sure what she felt. Yet deep inside she knew she liked hearing him say such things. Somehow it gave her a secret sense of pleasure to know that she could arouse him to a fever pitch of excitement that carried him over the edge each time they made love.

"By the way, Hal sends his regards. He'll be at your place this evening to bring us up to date on what's been happening since you last saw him," Damien informed her. "Is that time all right with you?"

"That will be fine," Trish murmured. "I'll call Gordy and have her fix enough for dinner so that Hal can eat with us." After that she lapsed back into silence, her thoughts running over the last four days and the fact that not one single thing had happened that could be blamed on her attackers.

She'd learned, through Damien, that even Hal had been surprised by how quiet things were, considering the almost daily contact that had occurred up to that point. The return trip from Florida had been made in Damien's car, with him driving. Nate had traveled behind in Trish's van with the dogs.

Her relationship with Damien had remained stormy during the days, only to smolder with passion at night. She no longer tried to remain aloof from his touch in the quiet, dark moments they shared. The time when he would leave her hung heavy on her mind, creating in her an insatiable appetite for his caresses that brought her embarrassment in the harsh light of day but glowing murmurs of approval from him at night.

"I think that must be Millie staring at us through the window," Damien said, breaking into her troubled thoughts. "Don't you think we should go in and let you introduce me?"

Trish almost bolted from the car, her hurried movements bringing a gleam of satisfaction to the azure depths of Damien's eyes as he followed her inside.

Any prayers Trish might have uttered in hopes of her partner reacting calmly to a brief recounting of what had happened in Florida, certainly had fallen on deaf ears.

"Do you mean to tell me that *he*"—pointing to Damien—"has been with you the entire time you were in Florida?" Millie demanded to know.

"Yes." Trish nodded, refusing to look at the tall figure propped against a table that held several thick books of wallcoverings. "Why?"

"Because I've been going out of my mind with worry, that's why," Millie said in a firm voice. "This place was broken into two nights ago. I also tried on two different evenings to call you, but I didn't get an answer."

"I'm afraid that's my fault, Millie," Damien spoke up. "I thought it best if Trish stayed with me. My brother Nate stayed in her room. He must have been out to dinner when you called."

"Well, the next time you decide to step in and change everyone's plans, how about letting someone know?" she snapped, not in the least daunted by the size of the man she was raking over the coals. She turned back to Trish, a look of pity showing in her attractive face. "It must have been horrible."

"It was—different, to say the least," Trish said, grinning. She walked over and sat on the edge of one of the high stools at a table. "So, tell me what Sergeant Decker's reaction was to the break-in you mentioned. I assume you reported it?"

"I could have saved my breath for all the good it did me." The small brunette frowned. "He brushed it off by implying that it was probably the work of some of the summer kids, looking for something to do. How does that grab you?"

"Not very nicely," Trish said, frowning. "But then, you must remember that I've had the pleasure of dealing with that incompetent weasel on a steady basis during the last three months."

"I think it's time for me to pay Sergeant Decker a little visit," said Damien, surprising both women. "Will one of you kindly direct me to his office?"

Without hesitating Millie grabbed Damien by the arm, marched him over to the window, and then pointed out the narrow brick building at the end of the street where the island's municipal offices were located. "And if you don't like the way he talks, which you won't, mash him," Millie ordered as she turned and rushed off to answer the phone.

Damien walked over to Trish and dropped a quick kiss on her startled lips. "I think we should arrange to have Millie come face-to-face with your 'friends.' Is she always so forceful?" he asked, chuckling.

"Only when she's annoyed. Other times she's as docile as a lamb." Trish smiled. A sudden sparkle shone in her eyes as an idea occurred to her. "I wonder what Nate would think of Millie?"

"Being rather kinky, he'd probably go for her in a big way," Damien said, grinning, then grunted when Trish tapped him in his solar plexus.

"I resent having my best friend and my—and a really great guy referred to as kinky." She gave him an evil look and hoped he hadn't noticed her momentary slip of the tongue.

"Don't get too fond of my little brother, sweetheart." Damien scowled. "You should know by now that I'm jealous as hell." He kissed her again, and then, with the reminder that there were agents behind every damn tree and probably in the bathroom, he left.

Trish remained seated, watching through the window as Damien's long, determined stride carried him up the old-fashioned cobblestoned sidewalk to Sergeant Decker's office. With the shop situated as it was, she had a bird's-eye view of the main street in the tiny municipality. She devoutly hoped Damien would give her the opportunity of seeing Sergeant Decker thrown out the front door of his office and into the street.

"Has he gone?" Millie asked in a stage whisper as she hurried up front, her hands busy replacing the earring she'd taken off when she'd answered the telephone.

"Yes," Trish whispered back, her eyes brimming with mischief. "Why?"

"How can you make jokes when your life is in danger?" Millie asked incredulously.

"Because after a while, my dear, you manage to overcome your fear and find yourself angry. I'm to the point I'd dearly love to meet my assailants. I do believe I could beat the hell out of them without any help at all."

"Count me in," Millie said stoutly. "I'd love to get a poke at them. But what about this Hal person you mentioned earlier. Does he have any idea what all this is about?"

Trish dropped her gaze to her hands, as if she had suddenly become inordinately interested in her fingers. "Ah, he mentioned one or two things, but neither of them made any sense," she answered unconcernedly.

"Trish"—her pint-size partner uttered her name in a tone of voice that brought a smile to Trish's face—"you're evading the issue and I want to know why. Have you forgotten that I've stood by you through this entire fiasco? That I was frightened out of my wits when I came in here two days ago and found the shop a wreck?"

The part about being frightened out of her wits brought a grin to Trish's face. Millie had never been frightened in her entire life. Her humor was short-lived, however, when Trish remembered Hal's warning not to involve her friends.

"There's an old saying, Millie: 'What you don't know won't hurt you.' I've never bothered to follow that particular adage, but in this case I think you would be wise to. The people we're dealing with wouldn't hesitate to harm you if they thought it would benefit them."

"I want to know the whole story," Millie stated firmly.

"They could easily slip into your apartment and slit your throat."

"Talk!"

"The Drug Enforcement Agency, for whom Hal Langdon works, suspects my father of smuggling drugs," she began, ignoring Millie's startled gasp. "Not puny little things like marijuana or a few pills, mind you. Dad, according to Hal, was up to his neck in cocaine. As best as we can figure, whoever is after me apparently thinks I still have a shipment. That would account for their incessant demands for me to return their merchandise."

"My God," Millie said weakly. She dropped into a nearby chair, her face deathly pale.

Trish gave her a worried frown. "Are you all right?"

"No, and I quite likely won't ever be again. No wonder they've been so insistent. Do you have any idea of the street value of cocaine?"

"I didn't until Hal informed me what it was. Apparently the stash I'm supposed to have absconded with goes well into the millions." Trish got to her feet. "Would you mind terribly if we dropped the subject, Millie? Find me some work to do—anything."

Millie willingly obliged, and when Damien stormed through the front door of the shop some forty-five minutes later, Trish was up to her elbows adding new wallpaper samples to the books.

"No wonder John's murderer was never found," he raged. "That damn Decker is about as competent as a nearsighted jackass!" The momentum of his anger carried him around the confines of the shop like a madly spinning top.

Trish and Millie glanced at each other, then back to Damien. "Er . . . was he rude to you?" Trish finally found the courage to speak. She had seen Damien in angry moods before, but this was the worst of the lot.

"Not after I grabbed that fat bastard by the front of his shirt and threatened to beat the living hell out of him right there on the spot," he snapped.

"How wonderful!" Millie exclaimed, her bright smile reflecting her enjoyment at even the thought of such a thing happening.

"Are you sure that was a wise thing to do?" Trish asked in a quieter voice.

"No, I'm not." Damien jerked around and faced her. "And when Hal hears about it, I'm sure he'll give me hell. But after sitting and listening to that fool make all sorts of wild accusations against John, I saw red."

"What did our esteemed constable say that finally made you want to clobber him?" the ever-curious Millie hurriedly asked.

In spite of his rage Damien gave her a half-hearted grin. "He made some unkind remarks about Trish and called you a witless featherhead."

"That pig," Millie hissed like a small kitten that's had its fur ruffled. "I wish I were a man," she said passionately. "I'd tar-and-feather that twit, then ride him out of town on a rail."

Damien walked over to her and dropped an arm casually around her shoulders. His face was now more relaxed, and a grin was on his lips. "Before you do that, Millie, why don't you let me introduce you to my baby brother? He's almost as large as I am, and he is rather partial to gals with spirit."

"Is he rich, or do you hold the purse strings?" the ever-practical Millie asked without blinking an eye.

"He's his own man in every sense of the word, I assure you," Damien said. "Shall I send him over later this afternoon?"

"But of course," Millie said, grinning impishly. "And don't worry"—she patted Damien's arm—"I'll take excellent care of him. In the meantime I have some phone calls to make."

After she'd gone back to the small office, Damien turned to Trish, who had been watching and listening with open amusement. "Poor Nate." He shook his head as he walked over to the large table and idly poked at the samples. "He'll probably want to kill me."

"Don't worry." Trish laughed. "I've complete faith in Millie. She puts up a good front, but when it comes to marriage, she runs like crazy. She was once married to a man who went beyond humiliating her; he tried to destroy her."

"Is that how you remember me, Trish?" Damien asked harshly.

"No," she said quickly, then swung around on the high stool, her knees pressing against his warm thighs. She reached up and cupped his face with both hands, her thumb gently gliding over the sensual fullness of his bottom lip. "Oh, no," she repeated softly. "We argued and fought and stormed at each other until we broke up our marriage, but it was done together, Damien. You never humiliated me, and I know you would never allow anyone else to do so, either."

"God, I love you, Trish," he groaned as he folded her into his arms, his legs parting so that her thighs slipped neatly between his and their hips were pressing tight against each other.

"I know," she whispered, "I know." But not any deeper than I love you, she thought. She wanted desperately to say those words, but she didn't have the courage. Once she said them, she knew Damien would never let her go. He'd been there for her when she needed him, and still was. He had welcomed her without a second thought when she was in trouble. It was becoming more and more apparent to Trish that any future she might have would have to include Damien.

"Why on earth do you want to meet my neighbors?" Trish asked some time later as Damien hustled her into the car.

"Orders," he answered tersely.

"Whose orders?"

"Old buddy Hal," he informed her. "He wants us to stick to the game plan." He gave her a measured look. "Isn't that sweet of Hal?"

Trish didn't comment. Instead she gave him directions, confused by the change that had swept over him. One minute he was holding her in his arms, telling her that he loved her. The next he was acting as if the very sight of her set his teeth on edge. Was Hal's constant urging him to marry her beginning to make Damien have second thoughts?

CHAPTER SIXTEEN

"I wasn't aware that you were planning on selling your place, Trish," Wyatt Jamison remarked as he accepted the cup of coffee Trish handed him.

"Actually, Wyatt, she wasn't planning to, were you, darling?" Damien smiled lovingly at her. "But after we're married we'll be living in Texas on my ranch. I think it would be best to sell the property rather than let it stand vacant. Of course, renting it is out of the question."

They were sitting in Wyatt's attractive living room, and Trish was having one heck of a battle with herself to keep from hurling the cup of hot coffee she was holding straight at Damien's detestable head.

"I can certainly understand your not wanting to let the house remain vacant," Wyatt said, frowning. "On the other hand, if you could be persuaded to rent I'd be more than happy to act as your agent."

"I'll keep that in mind," Trish spoke up, flashing Wyatt a grateful smile. "After all, Damien can't know how jealously we guard every inch of land here on the island, can he?"

"Indeed not," Wyatt agreed, then went on to explain in great detail the fear most of the local residents had of seeing their beloved island turned into a vacation spot. "A number of the families presently living here inherited their property." He looked at Trish. "As you did. Your father often expressed the hope that you would stay."

"Even so," Damien said coolly, "I doubt John would have wanted us to be saddled with property we'd never use. The likelihood of us ever coming back to Shoppal is very slim."

Not only was Damien an expert liar, Trish thought as she listened to him tell one whopper after the other, but he'd also turned into the royal fool of the year the instant Wyatt had hugged Trish and kissed her on the cheek. At that precise moment, she'd thought she'd seen smoke curling upward from his ears when Wyatt kept his arm around her as he ushered them into the house.

Now he was sitting next to her on the sofa, spouting off like some insufferable twit. His actions were completely out of line, she told herself. Wyatt Jamison had been friends with her father since Trish had been in grade school. The two men had played chess on a regular basis for years. When tragedy struck, Wyatt was one of the first to rush to her side.

After enduring Damien's actions for as long as she could, Trish looked sweetly at her "betrothed" and gave him a sugary smile. "I hate to break this up, darling, but don't you think it's time we were leaving? Gordy will be furious if we let that delicious casserole she left for us in the oven burn."

"I'm so glad you were able to convince Mrs. Gordon to come back and help you out," Wyatt remarked pleasantly. "It will seem like old times having her around the place. Oh"—he placed a detaining hand on Trish's arm—"I almost forgot. I would like to host a small party for you and Damien. Even though it's your second marriage to each other, I see no reason why there shouldn't be festivity surrounding the event."

"Thank you." Trish got in before Damien could say something insulting. "But I'm afraid we can't let you do that. Our plans are still rather uncertain at the moment."

"Well, if you can decide on a date give me a call. I hope it works for you two this time," he said quietly as they walked toward the door.

Trish was touched by his sincerity and said so the moment they were in the car, directly after telling Damien in a scathing tone that he had the manners of a pig.

"Need I tell you exactly what you can do with your good manners, my dear?" he retaliated, "along with your 'dear friend' Wyatt. In my opinion he's nothing but a lecherous old fool. He could barely keep his slimy hands off you."

"You are impossible, Damien St. Clair," she yelled at him. "Absolutely impossible."

Thankfully the other short calls they paid on several more neighbors went more smoothly. The difference in Damien's personality amazed Trish. He was charming; he was solicitous. She knew that left each of her neighbors and friends with the feeling that Trish was a lucky girl to be marrying her rancher again. Some of them remembered Damien from before and were pleased to renew their acquaintances with him.

"How was I so lucky to miss meeting dear Wyatt during our visits when we were married?" Damien asked as they were driving back home.

"He travels extensively," Trish answered shortly. He still had a long way to go before she forgave him. "He has an antique shop in Savannah and is frequently away on buying trips."

"What a pity he happened to be home today."

"I do believe I hate you," Trish muttered in

a deadly calm voice, unable to believe the screwy workings of his pea-size brain.

"That's great, sweetheart," he said roughly. "If hating me causes you to respond the way you do in my arms at night, then hate me some more."

That remark silenced Trish for the remainder of the ride home. For he spoke the truth, and no amount of denying it could erase that fact.

Not only did Hal arrive promptly at the appointed hour, but also he was in possession of news that brought tears to Trish's eyes.

Through information given by a man picked up in a drug bust in Miami, Shoppal Island had been mentioned. One of the agents sharing in the questioning knew that Hal was working on that particular location and channeled the information to him. Further checking revealed that the person responsible for getting the cocaine to Shoppal was Michael Tolar, Trish's father's assistant, not John Sanders.

"Thank you, Hal," Trish said quietly, clinging to Damien's reassuring hand. Her lips trembled with emotion, and her vision was blurred as she looked at him. "I never once doubted Dad's innocence."

"Believe me, Trish, I share your happiness," Hal told her. "In my job it's not often that I get the chance to bring someone good news."

"This calls for a celebration," Damien's deep voice cut in. He nodded to Nate, who got up and walked over to the fridge and took out a bottle of wine.

"I'm not so sure about this," Trish said, laughing as Nate set the stemmed glass before her. "The last time I decided to have a drink, I wound up with some creep trying to strangle me—and a horrible hangover the next morning."

"The hangover was the result of you making a pig of yourself over margaritas," Nate said close to her ear in a smirking tone. "Tonight I'm the bartender, squirt, and you'll be limited to one innocent glass of wine."

"Fink."

"In the flesh."

"If you 'kids' can manage to cut out the cute little remarks, Hal would like to get on with the rest of what he came to tell us," Damien spoke grimly, his gaze pinned on Nate's hand resting on Trish's shoulder.

"Your fangs are showing, brother dear," Nate returned in an equally tight voice. "If you don't get a grip on that damned jealousy, you're liable to wind up a withered old man all by yourself."

"Why don't you give me a refill, Nate," Hal said in an effort to change the topic of conversation. "Then there are a couple of other little tidbits of information I think Trish will appreciate."

Once the tense moment had passed and Hal was once again in control of the conversation, Trish realized that she had been holding her breath. Without any outward show of emotion, she slowly exhaled. Out of the corner of her eye, she could feel the full blast of Damien's gaze. She turned her head slightly and met his eyes. Without a word passing between them, Trish felt the secret hidden deep in her heart burst from its prison, shining through her eyes and reaching out to him in silent entreaty. A slight quiver touched her lips when she saw his look of puzzlement. Then, slowly, a dazed, almost stunned expression came over his face, and finally a gentleness softened his features. Trish ached to feel his arms around her. It took a light kick on her shin from Nate to break the spell that bound her in a velvet grip.

"We've dug up some very interesting background material on Sergeant Decker," Hal said, glancing at Trish as he talked, his mouth quirking humorously as he spoke. "It seems that he was 'allowed' to resign from the police force in a large city in the Midwest. We're still working on that, and I'll let you know more as soon as I hear. At any rate, after not being employed for about nine months, he suddenly turned up as constable on Shoppal. An interesting point about his appointment is that Wyatt Jamison, who just happens to have made a number of trips to the city where Decker previously lived, was the main one on the council pushing for Decker to get the job."

"Surely 'Uncle' Wyatt couldn't be involved," Damien interjected smoothly, refusing to look at Trish.

Nate gave a snort of a laughter at Damien's words just as Hal continued speaking.

"From what we've been able to piece together, and after adding our own speculation, this is what we've come up with. It looks as though Tolar, totally without John Sanders's knowledge, was the one responsible for bringing in and getting out certain large shipments of cocaine. The dog shows were a perfect cover. How he managed to hide each shipment is still a mystery. Who would think to suspect one of several assistants to a professional handler of smuggling dope? It was a setup made in heaven, because it involved unlimited travel all over the United States and to several foreign countries. We also believe Decker was one of his accomplices here on the island."

"I'll say this for you, my friend. You really know how to hold one's attention," Damien said approvingly. "As much as I detest

Decker, I doubt I'd ever have suspected him."

"Neither would I," Trish admitted. "I merely considered him some sort of bungling incompetent. Will you arrest him?"

"Oh, no," Hal said, shrugging. "We only suspect him of being involved, Trish. We haven't got one single shred of evidence to nail him with. If Tolar were alive, well, we could put a tail on him and grab him. But for the moment all we can do is hope somebody, somewhere, will slip up. That's why I want you to be as visible as possible. Make sure the news of your supposed engagement and pending marriage to Damien is well known. If the thugs that have been causing you so much trouble get wind of this latest development in your personal life, perhaps they'll panic. At least that's what we're hoping for."

"You mentioned that you thought Decker was only one of two accomplices on the island. Why do you think that? Do you have any idea who the other one is?" Nate asked.

"Our songbird in Florida," Hal said, grinning, "didn't come right out and point a finger at Decker, but he sure as hell hinted strong enough. But even *he* didn't know the identity of the other person involved. From what he'd heard from Tolar it was a man, and a respected member of the community."

"You mentioned that Wyatt Jamison was instrumental in securing Decker's present position," Damien cut into the discussion. "You are checking him out carefully, aren't you?"

"I am checking him out, and frankly I think he's the brains behind the entire operation here on the island."

"That's incredible!" Trish exclaimed. "It's hard to believe that someone I've known practically all my life could be responsible for what's happened to my family."

"Unfortunately, Trish, you're living under the misconception that anyone remotely connected with drugs, prostitution, or gambling will look like a crook. That's not the way it is, honey. We've moved into a sophisticated era of crime, involving people from every walk of life, where men who are considered pillars of the community can, and quite often are, leading double lives."

"That's frightening," Trish murmured. "Aren't they afraid of the consequences if they are found out?" she asked curiously.

"The amount of money involved makes it worth it. Most of them have cultivated a certain circle of friends and live on such a grand scale that they can ignore the risk they're taking. They become victims of their own greed."

Damien looked at Trish. "You certainly have to agree that Wyatt lives on a grand scale, honey. Even to my untrained eye the antiques and paintings in his home looked to be worth a fortune."

"Really, Damien." Trish glared at him. "Don't you think you're letting your personal feelings for the man get a little out of hand? Helping someone get a job is hardly a crime."

"Hal?" Damien said curtly.

Hal threw Trish an apologetic grin. "Sorry, honey, but at the moment almost everyone on this island is a suspect. The number of trips Jamison makes each year would be an excellent cover. We'll know more when our investigation is complete. There is one aspect of the case that still has us puzzled, though, and that's your father's death. Personally I think it was a freak accident. No one in his right mind would deliberately sabotage an arrangement such as they had going."

"Do you suppose Mr. Sanders was mistaken for someone else?" Nate asked. He leaned forward, his arms resting on the edge of the table. "Let's look at what we *think* we know. Tolar was bringing the shipments back to Shoppal. Since the kennel and this house have been searched repeatedly since Mr. Sanders's death, I think we can safely assume the stuff was usually hidden on his property, probably the kennel. Tolar would have had little difficulty hiding something there for a short period of time. He had the run of the place. At night, or when Trish's dad and his staff were away at shows, Tolar's accomplice would slip in, retrieve his merchandise, and leave. In my opinion, the foul-up came when Tolar was killed and Mr. Sanders returned home unexpectedly. From then on it became a game of chance, and whoever was picking up the cocaine knew that his chances of getting caught were far greater."

"I agree." Hal nodded approvingly. "If you ever get tired of putting up with your brother, you can come work for me."

"No, thanks," Nate hastily declined the offer. "I don't like the game plan."

"Where does that leave us now?" Damien asked.

"A hell of a lot closer to solving this mystery than we were three days ago," Hal told him. "I have this gut feeling that all hell's about to break loose. You stay with Trish at all times," he instructed Damien. "If you have to leave her then make sure Nate is with her. My men are all over this island. There's even two of them in a small cabin cruiser anchored in the bay directly across the road from the front of this house. But it's still imperative that we keep out of sight."

"In other words, Trish is still the bait, isn't she?" Damien bit out the words in a harsh voice.

"Yes, she is." Hal met Damien's eyes without apology. "You of all people should know

218

what goes down in an investigation of this sort, Damien. I'm sorry Trish is involved, but unfortunately we weren't consulted when that decision was made. Nothing we can do or say will make them believe she isn't hiding that damned shipment of cocaine. And until it's found we have no other recourse but to go on as we've been."

Later, after Hal had gone and they were walking hand in hand along the stretch of beach across the road from the house, Trish tried to calm the fear for her safety she knew Damien was experiencing. "You do understand why it has to be this way, don't you?" she asked.

"No," he snapped, his grip on her hand tightening.

"Certainly you do." She smiled tenderly. "Because of those people, whoever they are, my father lost his life. Wouldn't you feel the same way if it were Nate or Barb? Wouldn't you have to know who was responsible?"

A rough sigh of frustration rushed from Damien's lips as he stared out over the bay. "Yes, I'd have to know," he finally admitted. "But this situation is slightly different, sweetheart. I'm afraid I'll lose you."

Trish stopped, her hands going to his face and forcing him to look at her. "Nothing will happen to me, Damien," she softly murmured. "Believe me. I have to do this, because running away and hiding is unthinkable. My father's memory deserves better."

She had reason to remember those words the following day, when Gordy called her at the shop and told her that Jester was seriously ill.

Within minutes a white-faced Trish jumped from the car the moment Damien screeched to a halt in the driveway. "How is he?" she asked a worried-looking Nate, who was kneeling beside the large white poodle. She dropped to her knees beside the inert Jester and gently raised his head to rest in her lap. "He acts as though he's been poisoned," she said to no one in particular.

"Let us have him, honey." Damien came down beside her. "Right now he needs to be gotten to the vet."

Trish found herself numb with fear as she sat in the backseat of the car with one hand on Jester's muzzle while Damien broke all speed limits across the causeway to Savannah and to John Abbott's office. Once there, the awful waiting continued as the vet worked to revive the unconscious dog and also to try to determine exactly what had happened to him.

"I thought when I put the poodles on the sun porch that no one could get at them," Trish muttered as she paced the tiled floor of the waiting room. "It occurred to me after the phone calls began that they were open targets in the kennel. What do you do when your own home is no longer safe? Where on earth do you go then?"

"Stop it, Trish." Damien's voice sounded harsh and severe under the circumstances, but it had the desired effect. Trish turned on him, anger plainly visible in her sad eyes. But before she could say anything, John Abbott appeared in the doorway.

"You can relax" were the first words he said to the two anxious people who turned to greet him. He walked into the room and sat down on one of the leather-covered benches that lined the brick wall. "It's the darndest thing I've ever seen." He shook his head, clearly baffled. "Jester isn't near death, Trish; in fact, far from it. That poor bugger is on a high that would be the envy of every addict in the state were they to see him."

"High?" Trish exclaimed, staring incredulously at the man. "But he seemed so lifeless. I thought he was dying."

"And so might he, tomorrow when he begins to wake up. In the meantime, put your worries aside. Just make sure your other two dogs don't find old Jester's little treasure trove or they'll also be drunk as skunks."

"Can you identify the substance?" Damien asked casually, so casually that Trish frowned. What on earth was the matter with him? Trish asked herself.

"I really can't say at this point. But I'll know in a couple of days. I suggest you leave him here till then, Trish. Okay?"

"Okay." She smiled weakly, her knees beginning to shake now that her worst fears had been laid to rest. She followed Damien unresistingly to the car, almost sick with relief.

"Feeling better now?" he asked as he eased the car out of the parking lot and into the steadily moving traffic.

"Unbelievably so." Trish sighed. "But I keep trying to figure out what Jester could have gotten hold of. I've never had anything like this happen before."

When they got back home, the first thing Trish saw as she walked in was Gordy sweeping the sun porch as if the hounds of hell were nipping at her heels. After being told that Jester would be all right the elderly woman got right down to business. "Your father, God rest his soul, almost drove me crazy with all that powder and cornstarch he used on those terriers. But I never dreamed you'd come along and do the same thing."

"What on earth are you talking about, Gordy?" Trish asked.

"Well, just look at this mess," the former housekeeper pointed to the fine, white film of dust surrounding the three wooden crates where the poodles stayed. "It's the second time today I've had to sweep it up. Every time they come in out of the runs or leave these crates, they shake and mess up my floor."

"But I don't use powder on the poodles, Gordy," Trish said, trying to pacify the woman.

"That's what Wyatt Jamison told me, but I didn't pay any attention to him. Imagine him trying to tell me something about show dogs."

"Jamison?" Damien repeated sharply. "Was he over here?"

"He sure was. Came right after you and Trish went flying off to the vet. He never did say what he wanted, just sort of hung around here on the porch while I swept. When I told him about Jester getting hold of some kind of poison, he ran out of here like a shot. I figured he was going to Dr. Abbott's office to see you."

"Where's Nate?" Damien asked.

"At the kennels," Gordy said, frowning. "I don't for the life of me understand that young man, Damien. He's been prowling around out there all day as though he's searching for something. The only time he takes a break is when he comes in to eat."

"Nate doesn't get along too well with strangers, Gordy," Damien lied with a straight face. He turned to Trish. "Go tell Nate about Jester, and be sure to stay with him," he murmured in a low voice. "I'm going to see Hal."

"About what?" Trish asked as she followed him outside.

"I'm not even sure myself," he answered, a thoughtful frown pulling at his lip. "It's just a hunch I want to run by Hal."

CHAPTER SEVENTEEN

Apparently Damien's hunch hadn't proved valid, or that's what Trish assumed. He didn't mention it again, and she didn't probe. They were both under a tremendous strain, and she found herself trying to keep the investigation from being the only thing discussed.

It was the third day since she'd been home, and she found herself itching to get back into her old routine. She said as much to Damien bright and early that morning, while they were involved in the delicate game of trying to peep around each other in the mirror that hung in the bathroom.

"If you weren't as big as a mountain I could do this better," she grumbled as she jockeyed for a position beneath his raised arm.

"Mmmm." He eyed her cockily through the foam of shaving cream that covered a good portion of his face. "I don't recall you having any such complaints last night."

"Last night I wasn't trying to put on my

makeup," she retorted sharply. "Being jostled while applying eye shadow isn't one of the highlights of my day."

The next thing she knew, Damien had grabbed her by the back of her head and was kissing her pouting lips, the minty fragrance of his white shaving cream adding a comical touch to her cheeks and chin.

"That was a rotten thing to do!" she cried out at him as she stared at herself in the mirror. "Now I have to start all over again."

"What a shame." Damien grinned at her in the mirror. His hands had found their way to the inviting line of her hips and were slipping like quicksilver over the satin-covered skin.

Trish tried to ignore the quick surge of desire springing to life within her at his touch. She jerked a tissue from the box on the vanity and began rubbing at her face.

"You shouldn't be so heavy-handed, sweetheart," her tormentor murmured in her ear, his head dipping close to hers at the same time he was molding the slight curve of her buttocks against the familiar hardness of his thighs, leaving her in little doubt of his own arousal.

"I wouldn't have to be if a certain rat fink hadn't seen fit to smear shaving cream all over my face."

"This is the damndest piece of lace and satin I've ever encountered." He scowled as his hands were met with soft resistance at every turn. "What the hell is it?"

"It's called a teddy, you sap," Trish said, grinning. She wiggled her bottom sensuously against his towel-covered thighs. "Don't you like it?" Her voice became a velvet purr of seduction. The thought of redoing her makeup was suddenly not quite as important as it had been only seconds ago.

"No." Damien came near to gasping, his fingers biting into the lower part of her abdomen as a shudder hit his frame. His fingers feathered their way upward and then slipped the thin, fragile straps from her shoulders.

The weight of the alluring garment caused it to slide effortlessly to her waist, baring her breasts to Damien's touch. She saw the color of his eyes darken with desire as his thumbs began an exciting manipulation of the tiny nipples that crowned each creamy mound.

Suddenly the weight of her head seemed too much to bear. She let it relax against his chest, the tip of her tongue running over the dry surface of her parted lips. "I—I think I'm going to be late," she managed just as his hands disappeared beneath the satin covering and smoothed the shadowy triangle at the top of her thighs.

"Correction, sweetheart," he said softly. "You definitely *are* going to be late, because I'm going to make love to you."

Damien pulled the towel loose from his hips, then bent and swung her up into his arms. He carried her to the bed, laying her against the rumpled sheets, then grasped the teddy and removed it.

Trish opened her arms to him, impatient for him to take her. When he complied with her unspoken plea and entered her, she bit back a cry of pleasure. She clasped him to her, the crisp growth of hair on his chest acting like some wild, erotic stimulus against the excited tips of her breasts.

Their journey into paradise was short, the depth of their individual passions leaving them incapable of such mundane notions as restraint. When the final cry of fulfillment burst from Damien's lips, he crushed Trish in his arms, carrying her with him over the edge.

"Making love to you is getting to be a habit. What am I going to do when you no longer need a bodyguard?" he asked some time later as he dropped a kiss on her forehead, then took the edge of the sheet and tickled the end of her nose.

Trish pushed herself into a sitting position, a frown suddenly appearing on her face. "According to the last letter I got from Barb, you haven't been doing too badly. I distinctly remember her mentioning something about your old friend Lauren Poole being a frequent visitor to the ranch these days."

This surprising comment had Damien wanting to choke his meddlesome sister. For even if he had fallen back into his old relationship with Lauren, it would mean nothing if he had a chance of getting Trish back.

"At the time there didn't seem to be any reason for me not to see her," he said, finally breaking the silence that had crept over them.

"Did you make love to her?" Trish asked him, then braced herself for the answer.

"Are you sure you want to know?"

"Yes, I want to know!" she snapped. "It's beginning to look to me as though you're like one of those damn bulls on your ranch. You ramble fat, dumb, and happy from one woman to the other."

"Damn"—he grinned outrageously, his spirits soaring in the face of her anger—"you make me sound like some pervert."

"You are." Trish glared at him, the flood of jealousy that swept over her leaving even the tips of her fingers tingling. "But you haven't answered my question," she said, smiling acidly. "Have you been spending the last few months making love to that witch Lauren Poole?"

Damien knew exactly how a trapped animal felt. He warily eyed Trish's angry expression and immediately sat up, then moved away until he was well out of reach of his "darling's" right hand. "Ahem . . ." He made a pretense of clearing his throat. "I—I suppose there have been one or two occasions upon which we were caught up in a moment of passion."

"One or two," Trish hooted scathingly. "Don't be ridiculous. I know you too well, Damien St. Clair. You've got the sexual appetite of ten men. I wonder just how many others have provided you with pleasant little tidbits, you deceitful bastard!"

Before he could move, she whipped the pillow from behind his back and whammed it down over his head, then jumped from the bed and flew to the bathroom.

After she'd flipped the lock into place on the door, she swung around, the blood pounding through her veins. She placed her palms against her throbbing temples and stared at her reflection in the mirror.

What had happened? she asked herself as the incredible scene she'd just made was replayed in her mind. She hadn't thought of Lauren Poole in days, not since that first night in Florida when she'd first run into Damien. Why now? Why had the picture of the statuesque redhead popped into her mind after Damien had just made love to her?

Was it because she knew he was free? That

their divorce had given him the right to live his life as he chose? she asked herself. She had told herself over and over that she didn't want him back, that she couldn't bear to take the risk of losing him all over again. But the prospect of another woman having him was just as shattering.

No amount of mental juggling brought forth the answer she was seeking. It was as though her mind had snapped. One minute, deliriously happy; the next, ready to commit murder in a jealous rage. And to cap it all off, she thought, sighing, she'd been in such a rush to make a fool of herself, she'd forgotten that her clothes were in the bedroom.

With her shoulders squared and her chin held at a haughty angle Trish flipped back the lock, opened the door, then walked nonchalantly into the bedroom.

Damien, who was still in the exact same spot as he had been when she'd left, watched her progress about the room as she went from closet to chest, gathering up her clothes for the day. For once in his life he found himself in a situation from which he hadn't the slightest idea how to remove himself. However, there was one thing he was certain of: He would never again admit to having made love to another woman during the three years they'd been apart, even if Trish held a gun to his head.

God! What a mistake he'd made with his asinine confession of "one or two times." He chewed thoughtfully at his bottom lip, trying to figure a way out of this mess. Just how to begin such an explosive conversation, however, was soon taken out of his hands.

"You may move your clothes into the guest room down the hall," Trish told him icily from the closet where she had slipped into a robe and was yanking the belt tightly around her waist.

"No," Damien said simply.

"Oh?" She whirled around and leveled her most quelling glance toward him before looking away. "Why not? Is the thought of being without sex so terrible that you can't bring yourself to sleep alone for a few more days?"

"Quite the contrary." He swung his legs to the floor and was halfway across the room before Trish caught the sound of his approach. Before she could scamper away, he wrapped his arms around her in a giant bear hug. He looked down into her mutinous face, his own features calm. "I intend staying right where I am, and so will you. I'm sorry if the answer you got hurt you, Trish. Lauren means nothing to me. If she did I could have married her anytime during the past three years. She was simply there at a time when I needed someone, and I used her. Just as she used me."

"But Barb said—"

"Knowing my sister and the illogical way her tiny brain works, she probably panicked. She's never been overly fond of Lauren."

Trish dropped her gaze, feeling foolish and rather dumb. "I don't know what came over me," she confessed.

"Neither do I, but I'm damn glad it happened."

"You're as dopey as I am." Trish eyed him curiously. "Why on earth are you happy to see me make a complete fool of myself?"

"Because it makes me know for certain that you still love me."

"Oh . . . is that all?" she asked pertly.

"Well, it sure as hell is important to me," he said, frowning. "I've been going around for days, banging my head against a stone wall trying to figure out how to make you admit it." He brushed back a silky strand of her hair with one large, gentle hand. "There's only one thing wrong with your little outburst."

"What?"

"Your timing is lousy. The aftermath of lovemaking is to be savored. It's something to let seep through the drugged corridors of one's mind. You ruined it just about as well as anyone possibly could."

"I was jealous." Trish looked him straight in the eye as she spoke. "Plus, knowing Hal suggested that you ask me to marry you has left me wondering if what has happened between us is real or simply a show."

"Oh, it's no show, honey; it's for real. As for your jealous outburst, I loved it. Only next time give me a word of warning. I do believe you raised a nice lump on my head." He then had the nerve to raise a hand to his head and rub at the nonexistent wound.

Trish sat at her desk in the small office in the back of the shop, her concentration broken from time to time by the sound of Millie and Nate arguing. It was too soon to tell, she thought with a smile, but from the way those two were going at each other, there just might be a new romance in her partner's life.

She looked at her watch, wondering where Damien was. He'd dropped her and Nate off at the shop, then left. The pen in her hand eased from her fingers as she leaned back in the chair and let her thoughts take over.

What was she going to do about Damien?

Being with him day and night for nearly two weeks had shown her that without him her life would be empty. His suggestion that she open another shop in Texas resolved the problem of her career being a trouble spot between them. But what about children? She raised the question to herself, the answer leaving her with a bleak, unhappy look on her face. Why was it so necessary for a man to leave an army of sons to carry on the family name, and in his case, the ranching tradition of the St. Clair empire? If he loved her as he said he did why couldn't he be content with just the two of them being together?

Tell him, the weary voice of her conscience pushed through the cluttered thoughts in her mind. He has a right to know that it's not your lack of love for children, but rather your awful fear of childbirth that keeps making you put him off. Damien will help you sort it all out, you know he will.

Trish closed her eyes against what she knew to be the truth, but the shame she felt because of her fear wouldn't release her. How, she asked herself, with all the wonders of modern medicine that were available, could anything possibly go wrong with a woman having a baby? How could she explain that knowing that her own mother had died in childbirth had left her with such a fear that she would break out in a cold sweat when she dwelled on the subject too long.

Yes, she told herself, she did want children. She would welcome a dozen sons with hair like Damien's. She smiled as she imagined him lying on the floor, tussling with tiny replicas of himself. But the smile faded as the cold hand of fear gripped her heart.

"Trish?" Nate's worried voice broke into her thoughts, causing her to give a start at the suddenness of the sound. "Are you all right?" He walked into the room and sat on one corner of the desk, clearly concerned.

Trish quickly brushed at her cheek with an unsteady hand, then began shuffling the papers in front of her. "I'm fine," she said without looking up.

Nate leaned forward and tucked one tanned forefinger beneath her chin, forcing her to meet his gentle gaze. "If you're fine then I'm a duck."

This ridiculous comparison brought a smile to her lips. "You're also something of a nut, and I adore you."

"And I, you. Now that we've disposed of that little matter, would you please tell me what's upset you? Are you anxious about the case?"

"It's not the case at all. It's something personal. I suppose you could say I was indulging in a little self-pity."

"Is Damien giving you trouble?"

"Not in the sense you mean." Trish smiled. "I will never forget how kind he's been through all this."

"There's the definite ring of finality in your voice," Nate said with a frown. "That's surprising, considering how close the two of you have been for days. Does Damien know you plan on dumping him the moment the investigation is over?"

236

Trish was startled by the accusing tone of his voice. Nate had always been so devil-may-care, a great big lovable teddy bear without a vicious bone in his body. At the moment, however, he was quite annoyed and making no effort to hide it.

"I wouldn't call it dumping him," she said, trying to defend herself and finding that she really didn't have a defense. "Damien isn't a little boy, Nate. He's known all along what our relationship would be."

"Come off it, Trish," he scoffed. "Have you forgotten that I'm living in the same house with you? I see the looks that pass between the two of you. I see the way you reach out to each other. I feel the love that charges between you the minute you come together."

"Well, then, look at it from another angle," she said sharply. "It really isn't any of your business, is it?"

"That's where you're wrong, squirt," Nate countered. "I saw you leave my brother once before, and it damned near killed him. And from all accounts you didn't fare too well from the experience either. It's a time in all our lives I'd like to forget. And I damn well don't want to see it repeated."

Without another word he got up and left the room, leaving a shattered Trish to stare after him. It was the first time she'd ever had a disagreement with Nate, she thought sadly,

237

but she couldn't blame him for trying to protect his brother.

The coolness between them continued as the afternoon wore on. When Damien arrived to take her home, there was a look of puzzlement on his rugged features at this surprising turn of events. His wife and his brother had always been allies, he thought as he watched. Now they were acting like polite strangers. He glanced at Millie, his brows raised in question, but all she did was to shrug her shoulders.

"Did you enjoy your first day back at work?" he asked Trish after kissing her and holding her hard against his chest for a brief moment as soon as they got in the car.

"It was so-so," she replied noncommittally, then lapsed into a brooding silence.

"Have you and Nate quarreled?"

"No."

"Was he ugly or insulting to you?"

"Of course not."

"Did you get another phone call from your friends?"

"No."

"Are you still angry at me because of Lauren?"

"Don't be silly."

"Then will you please tell me what the hell is the matter?" he yelled. "Getting information out of you is like getting water from a damn stone!"

"Nate and I had a discussion, during which he let me know in no uncertain terms that he didn't want me to hurt you again." Trish told him in a rush. "Now are you satisfied?" She glowered at him.

"I think it's time I had a word with that young man. I'm long past the stage where I need someone to wipe my nose."

"If you dare say a word to him I'll never speak to you again," she threatened. "He was only trying to protect you. I can't hold that against him."

"Then why were the two of you acting so cool toward one another?"

"Because he made me see some things about myself that I didn't find very pleasant. I'm human enough not to want to rush out and hug him. We'll work it out, though. There's no need for you to become involved."

Her chance for a few words alone with Nate came right before dinner while Damien was on the phone with Hal.

"I'm sorry for barking at you this afternoon," she said as she was dishing up the pot roast. Nate had set the table and was pouring iced tea into two glasses.

"Don't worry about it, honey. I was told off by your friend Millie rather royally." He gave

239

her a lopsided grin. "I shouldn't have come down on you so hard."

"You probably did me a favor," Trish said with a sigh. "There are some things between Damien and me that have never been discussed. Perhaps between now and the time he's ready to leave we can hash them out. At least that's what I'm planning on."

"That's the only way to go, kid," he said encouragingly. "Communication is the key to any successful relationship."

"Oh? Is that why you're still a bachelor?" Trish teased.

"Now you're being nosy," he told her in mock sternness.

"Of course, but I have an excuse. I'm a woman. You, on the other hand, are supposed to be above such things."

"I must say, it's nice to see the two of you talking to each other again," Damien announced as he strolled into the room. He took the platter containing the roast, carrots, potatoes, and onions from Trish and placed it on the table. "Why is the table set for only two?"

"Nate's taking Millie to dinner," Trish threw over her shoulder as she took perfectly browned rolls from the oven. "Isn't that nice?"

"Do you mind not discussing me as though I'm not present?" Nate said curtly. He turned

240

to Damien. "Don't you think it's nice that I'm taking bad-tempered Millie to dinner?"

"I'm fairly certain it will be an evening you will long remember," Damien solemnly intoned, his lips twitching with laughter.

Nate screwed his mouth up into a distasteful grimace. He thumped the large glasses of tea down on the table, then turned and headed for the door. Just before he passed through, he turned and looked at Trish. "If I suffer bodily harm at the hands of that pint-size menace, then just remember it was you that introduced us."

"If she harms a single hair on your worthless body, I'll personally sue her," Trish called after him, laughing as she sat down in the chair Damien was holding for her.

"This is nice, the two of us eating alone." He smiled across at Trish. "Let's do it more often." She knew there was an invitation in the remark, and for once she didn't shy away from it. Nate would have been astounded had he only known what he had accomplished by his rather brisk talk with her.

"I'd like that." She tried to keep the trembling out of her voice as she answered him. "But only if you promise not to gripe about my cooking."

"I promise only to heap generous words of praise on your shining head, even if I have to have my stomach pumped out," he said smugly, feeling like a man who had suddenly found the pot of gold at the end of the rainbow.

Trish reached out and tapped his knuckles with her knife. "Just for that smart remark you can't have any dessert."

"What is it?"

"Apple pie."

"I promise to heap generous words of praise on your shining head, regardless of what you place before me to eat. How's that?" he asked, mischief glowing in his blue eyes.

"It's an improvement. Just don't think I'm a pushover, though."

"Now why would I think that?" he murmured silkily, the hidden meaning in his words bringing a slight, rosy glow to Trish's cheeks. For not only was she a pushover where he was concerned, but he was also able to bend her to his will as easily as if she were a piece of limp spaghetti.

"By the way"—Damien took pity on her and changed the subject—"Hal will be over later. I don't know if there's been much change since last night, but he wants to talk, anyway."

"I'm glad." Trish flashed him a grateful look. "It makes the agony of waiting a lot easier, knowing that something's being done at last."

CHAPTER EIGHTEEN

"I hope you won't become impatient with my questions, Trish," Hal told her as he dropped into an overstuffed chair in the den. "But when I don't cover all bases, I have this nasty habit of waking up in the middle of the night chasing ideas around in my head like a merry-go-round."

"That's understandable. But before Damien joins us, there is one little question I'd like to ask you." Trish filled the cup she was holding with coffee and handed it to him.

"Shoot."

"Did you really suggest to him that he propose to me?"

Hal grinned. "I did, but I honestly didn't think he would do it. He was afraid that you weren't going to be very cooperative about him coming back to Shoppal with you. Suddenly the idea occurred to me that if certain people knew you were thinking of marrying Damien and leaving the island, we might get some results." He considered her thoughtfully for several seconds. "I might have suggested it, honey, but I had nothing to do with what he feels for you."

Before she could probe further, Damien came into the room, and the discussion became limited to the investigation.

"Tell me something about your housekeeper, Mrs. Gordon," Hal said as he drew a ragged note pad from his inside coat pocket.

"She talks incessantly," Damien remarked from his position beside Trish on the sofa.

"True," Trish agreed, "but I don't think that's what Hal wants to hear. Gordy began working for my father shortly after I was born. When I went away to college, she retired. With Dad being gone so much of the time, it seemed pointless having a full-time housekeeper. After that, he hired daily help two or three times a week. When Damien and I parted, I had an apartment in Savannah for the first year. Then, when Millie and I decided to go into partnership and open the shop, Dad asked me to move back here. The rest you know. Damien suggested I find someone to help out. I called Gordy from Florida, and she agreed to come back to work for a while."

"Tell me about Millie Ames. How long have you known her?"

"For most of my life. She was raised on the

island the same as me. After high school we went our separate ways, then wound up working at the same interior design shop. It didn't take us long to realize that our different styles complemented each other. We took a chance, and it's beginning to pay off. I'd trust my life to Millie, Hal."

"Would you make the same statement regarding her ex-husband?" he asked.

"I never met the man, but from what Millie's told me, I wouldn't trust him an inch."

"And Wyatt Jamison?"

"Yes, Trish, tell him about Wyatt," Damien said in a maddening voice.

Trish shot him an acid look, then turned back to Hal. "As I'm sure you've gathered by now, Damien and I are of two different minds regarding Wyatt. He's ready to believe the very worst, but I honestly can't believe he's capable of hurting anyone. He and Dad played chess once a week if their schedules permitted. I've always regarded him as an uncle."

After writing something in his notebook Hal asked her about the neighbors on either side. Trish explained that both parties were elderly. "Mr. Carson is so crippled with arthritis that he can barely get around, and Mrs. Calhoun is a widow in her late seventies. I'm afraid the idea of smuggling cocaine would send either of the poor dears into cardiac arrest."

The game of questions and answers continued till Trish felt as though every important event in her life was recorded in the tattered notebook Hal carried. She bitterly resented this intrusion into her private life that had been caused by some faceless individual.

She knew it would also take her a long time before she could find it in her to have the same trust she'd had in people before her father's accident.

While Damien saw Hal to the door Trish placed the dirty cups on a tray and carried them to the kitchen. She couldn't help but feel disappointed by the fact that Hal hadn't had any significant news to report. She tried to tell herself that he was facing an almost impossible task, but she was beginning to feel desperate.

Picking up on her mood the moment he came into the room, Damien asked if she'd like to go for a walk.

"Yes," she answered immediately, and he gave her a grateful smile. "Maybe the breeze blowing in off the water will help me get over this awful depression."

As they walked along the white, sandy beach, Trish wondered if her emotional low was due entirely to the lagging investigation; or perhaps it was partially caused by the nagging quiver of guilt because she had refused to have Damien's child. She'd deliberately let him assume she disliked children.

For three years she'd wrapped herself in a cloak of self-righteousness, ready to blame Damien for every argument, every little disagreement that had taken place in their marriage. She had pictured herself as the injured party for so long that it had become reality in her mind.

Her father had seldom discussed her marriage after her divorce. He simply shifted his routine as effortlessly as possible to include his daughter, then went about his business as before. Trish now began to wonder if she could have saved her marriage if she'd worked a little harder at it.

She thought back earlier to the rather stern lecture Nate had given her, and how she had finally realized that she hadn't been the only one to suffer. She'd always thought of Damien as being somehow invulnerable. She'd never tried to find his weak spots; she'd been too busy fighting him.

It came as something of a shock to Trish, as she walked alongside the tall, silent man who held her heart in his hands, that part of her inability to get along with Damien stemmed from her resentment of his strength. She chanced a quick glance upward, taking in the rigid line of his profile, seeing the proud set of his shoulders. My God! She felt almost faint. Why hadn't she realized it before?

In her unconscious quest to find a man different from her quiet, and at times brooding, father, she'd chosen a man she could lean on. At first it had been wonderful. But when Damien began pressing her to have a child, Trish began to hate that strength she'd at first been so attracted to. And because she felt she could never tell him the real reason she couldn't have a child, Trish destroyed her marriage.

"Have you sorted it out yet?" The question was unexpected, and Trish stumbled as Damien came to an abrupt halt. He turned her to face him, then slipped his arms around her, his hands locked behind her back. "I was beginning to think we were going to have to walk to Maine and back before you reconciled yourself to whatever it is that's eating at you."

A gentle smile settled over Trish's face as she let her gaze wander over Damien's features. "It's been a struggle, but I think I've licked it."

"Is it private, or would you like to share it?"

"I'm afraid it doesn't put me in a very pretty light," she said quietly.

"Self-examination can sometimes do that to a person." He removed one arm but kept the other around her shoulders as he started them back down the beach. "That's why most people refuse to do it. It takes strength and courage for an individual to be honest with his inner thoughts, honey."

"Is that how you see me, Damien? Strong and courageous?"

"Yes." His answer was decisive. "While I've been dreading the moment when you'd collapse, and have been standing ready to pick up the pieces, you've been rushing along, gathering momentum as you raced from one frightening episode to another. There have been moments when I've wished you were less independent and a little more clinging."

"You'd be surprised if I were to tell you that it's because of you that I've been able to get through this awful time, wouldn't you?" She looked up at him then, and smiled when she saw the look of puzzlement registered in his face.

"To be perfectly honest, yes. I never suspected you of doing anything because of me. You were always hell-bent on opposing everything I suggested."

"That was because I was afraid of you."

"Afraid?" he repeated. "Why?"

"You possessed certain qualities that I didn't." She rushed on, afraid even now that she couldn't tell him. "Didn't it ever occur to you to probe deeper into my reasons for not wanting to get pregnant?"

"I just naturally assumed it was because you

wanted a career. At least that's what you kept telling me. Was I terribly dense?"

"Incredibly so." Trish sighed. "And that's quite unlike you, I might add. It's not, nor has it ever been, my career that made me not want children." She stopped walking and turned so she could see the light of the moon shining directly on his face. This was her life she was dealing with, and she wanted no room for added doubt. "My mother died in childbirth. I've kept the fear bottled up inside me that someday the same thing would happen to me. It was something that I knew was inside me, but I never had to face it until we married and you began pressing me to have a baby."

For what seemed like an eternity he made no move to touch her, instead letting the steady, unflinching directness of his gaze reveal to her the sympathy, the understanding he felt for her. When he finally saw the tears fill her eyes, he reached for her, folding her into his arms, shielding her with his love.

Long moments passed as Trish absorbed the warmth emanating from him. She couldn't begin to predict the future, but she felt cleansed that in some small way she had absolved him of the burden of guilt she'd given him three years ago.

"Was I so intimidating that you felt you

couldn't confide in me?" he murmured against her hair, his voice gruff with emotion.

"Yes, but not in the manner you're thinking. I envied you that incredible ability you have of facing incredible odds and coming out the winner. In my mind's eye, I pitted myself against you and clung to my fear like a child clings to a security blanket. Eventually I came almost to hate you for making me feel so insecure. It never occurred to me to reach out and take some of that strength for myself."

"And now?" he asked, subdued.

"Well, at least I no longer have resentment mixed in with my love for you."

"Thank God for small favors," he murmured fervently. "If Hal's men weren't watching us from that damn boat anchored out there, I'd make love to you right here on the sand with the moonlight bathing your sweet body."

Trish felt her knees go weak with passion. "You don't hate me for being such a coward? For allowing my fear to wreck our marriage?"

"I could never hate you, honey. I might occasionally want to turn you across my knee and pound that beautiful behind of yours, but hate? Never." He made a restless movement with his hands, then caught her hand in his and began striding toward the house.

"What on earth is wrong?" she cried as she tried to keep up with his giant steps.

"I want to kiss you. I want to make love to you, and I'll be damned if I'll do it with a pair of binoculars trained on us."

And later, as Trish lay warm and sated in his arms, she knew his words hadn't been uttered carelessly. He'd brought tears of happiness easing down her cheeks with the unbelievably tender way in which he'd worshiped her body with his hands and whispered endearments that flowed like honey from his lips.

The next morning at breakfast, Nate looked from one smiling face to the other, a speculative gleam narrowing his gaze. "Do the two of you realize how silly you look sitting there with huge grins plastered on your ridiculous faces?"

"What's wrong, Nate? Did Millie punch a hole in that incredible ego of yours?" Damien drawled. He lifted his coffee to his lips and continued to regard his brother over the rim of the cup.

Nate gave them a good-natured grin and let his head tip to one side as he thought about the question. "She's—different. I don't think I've ever met anyone quite like her."

"Is that a compliment?" Trish asked curiously. She knew from experience that Millie was a master at being obnoxious when trying to hide her true feelings. Trish found herself hoping that something in Nate had struck a responsive chord in Millie's stubborn heart.

"When I decide, I'll let you know. Right now my head is still swirling. I'm still trying to absorb everything that took place."

"While you're absorbing, do you have any specific plans for this morning?" Damien asked.

"I'll be at the shop this morning, then here this afternoon. I searched the kennel from top to bottom yesterday and didn't find even a hint of anything. If nothing comes to light today I plan on starting on the grounds tomorrow with a nice sharp shovel," he remarked ruefully.

"Don't you dare." Trish met his teasing gaze across the table. "The last thing I need is a six-foot four-inch gopher plowing up my yard." She turned on Damien. "He's your brother, do something."

He pushed back his chair, then dropped a kiss on her lips. "As usual, my dear, I always steer clear of the little arguments between you and Nate. I have no fear that you're perfectly capable of handling the situation. You'd better hurry; you did promise to open up this morning, didn't you?"

Later that morning, even the confirmation of two new accounts failed to thrill Trish as it would have a few weeks earlier. Having to deal with the countless questions asked by the clients prevented her from devoting her every thought to Damien and the relationship that was steadily growing between them.

Millie was in Savannah, looking over a new office complex they'd been asked to bid on, and Nate was slowly driving Trish up the wall with his obvious boredom. After turning around at least a dozen times and finding him at her elbow, she eyed him with a mean-eyed glare and pointed to a chair. "Sit!"

"Have you forgotten that I'm supposed to be your faithful bodyguard?" He returned her glare with equal fervor.

"How can I? I can't take two steps without running over you. Unless you expect a spook to suddenly appear from between the pages of one of the wallpaper books, then I fail to see the need for such dedicated attention."

"Well, I'm bored, damn it," Nate said with a scowl, his lips poking out like a small boy's. "When will Millie be back?"

"I pray it will be soon." Trish moaned as she tore open an invoice and began going over it. "On second thought"—she grinned evilly at him—"considering that she knows you're waiting for her, she's liable to disappear for good."

"You and your partner are without a doubt two of the most contrary women I've ever run into," he told her haughtily. "You don't need protection; the two of you could quite easily get jobs as wardens in a prison."

Before Trish could come back with an equally comical insult, the door of the shop opened, and two women with three small children came in.

After spending the better part of an hour trying to help one woman decide which kind of wallpaper she wanted, and at the same time trying to keep the kids from destroying the shop, Trish finally sent the party on their way, armed with two of the huge books. But almost before the door closed, someone else came in. The pace was hectic with customers and the constant ringing of the phone. When she finally had time to glance at her watch, she was surprised to see that it was close to eleven o'clock.

She found herself wanting to hang the CLOSED sign on the front door, then sit quietly and rest. Unfortunately a shipment of drapery material arrived, which meant getting in touch with the seamstress who was going to make the draperies. Then Trish had to contact the man who installed carpet for the shop and pin him down as to when he could start on the job.

She was in the middle of working out the final arrangements when Damien walked in. Unable to stop and talk, she smiled at him as he kissed her, then waved him to a nearby chair beside his brother.

After making sure that Mr. Thomas could start laying the carpet the next day, Trish dropped the receiver onto the cradle, then turned to the two waiting men. "Will you please tell your obnoxious brother to carry his worrisome hide from these premises?" she said to Damien.

A quirk of amusement flickered across his tanned features as he looked from Trish to Nate. "Is he being unpleasant?"

"Having him dog my every step is like being followed by a grouchy bear."

"I'd give it serious thought before trying to reconcile with your former spouse, Damien, if I were you," Nate sourly remarked. "She's about as pleasant to be around as a tiger with a toothache." He rose to his feet. "I'm going. Tell Millie I'll call her later."

"Have you been busy this morning?" Damien asked after hearing the front door slam.

"Have I ever!" Trish sighed as she dropped down in the chair beside him. "It always turns out this way when there's only one of us here. But"—she gave him a pert grin—"that's what pays the rent. I really can't complain."

"I talked with Hal this morning. He's coming over this evening."

"Now you've really ruined my day. I adore

your friend, but I've just decided that I resent spending each evening answering an endless round of questions."

"I know, honey," the sympathetic timbre of his voice flowed over her like a soothing balm. "But it's necessary."

"I know," Trish gave in reluctantly. "By the way, I have to go by the vet and pick up Jester. Will that pose a problem for you?"

"None at all," he said, smiling pleasantly. "I'm entirely at your disposal."

"Oh, my." She grinned wickedly, noting with a certain satisfaction how relaxed he looked. The lines of tension that had strained his features for days were gone. "How would you like to be attacked in a public place?"

"I suppose I could bear up," he said, grinning, "but only if you promise to respect me in the morning."

Trish giggled at his ridiculous posturing, then let her head drop back against the chair. "You're impossible, but I love you," she said softly. "I must be slightly bonkers."

"Because you love me?" Damien asked in an injured tone.

"No. Because I'm so happy. There's somebody out there just itching to throttle me, and here I sit with a grin on my face and thinking what a glorious day it's going to be."

"Don't stop to analyze your feelings, sweetheart," Damien cautioned her. "You got rid of a whole lot of guilt last night. Guilt you'd been carrying around for years. It's only natural for you to feel relief."

"But without your faith and trust in me I don't think I could have done it. Plus," she went on, "my darling ex-brother-in-law's little scolding."

The telephone rang at that moment, and Trish went to answer, leaving a very troubled Damien to wrestle with his own feelings of guilt.

He wondered what her reaction would be when she learned that his convenient arrival in Florida was far from the innocent accident she thought it had been. Would she listen to his explanation and know that it had been his concern for her that had made him go? Would she believe him—or Hal—when he told her that his suspicion of her at first had arisen from the overwhelming evidence Hal had presented him with?

He got up and began to walk around the room, his hands jammed into his back pockets. His thoughts of what could happen brought a deep aching to his heart. For the first time ever, he and Trish were actually talking. This was not the superficial chitchat that sentenced a relationship to eventual failure, but honest talking. Hearing her bare her soul to him last night had created such a wealth of happiness in him that he'd thought his chest would explode with joy.

One large hand left his pocket and went to the back of his neck, the fingers pressing into his skin. He'd never dreamed she'd been keeping such fear locked within her. And, he thought wisely, it's still there, but with understanding and patience he was confident he could help her overcome her misgivings about having a baby. Unfortunately he was also well aware of Trish's intense pride. Knowing he'd tricked her might well destroy any chances he had of building a life with her.

Jester came bouncing over to his mistress, his tail wagging like crazy as he reared up on his back legs and gave her several generous slurps with his pink tongue.

"Enough." Trish laughed as she caught his front legs and dropped them to the floor. "He looks wonderful." She smiled gratefully at John Abbott.

"He should," the friendly vet said, "he's certainly had enough rest. I'm sorry for the delay in the test results, Trish. As soon as they come in I'll give you a call."

"Thanks, John." She handed the leash to Damien, then followed him and Jester to the car.

"Wow!" she exclaimed as she relaxed

against the seat. "I'm relieved to see him so perky."

"Can you ever remember anything like this happening to any of the dogs your dad showed?" Damien asked.

"Never. There've been occasions when one of the dogs would decide to go after a frog, but nothing like what Jester got hold of. Personally I think he was given something. Nothing to kill him, mind you. But strong enough to knock him out. I think it was a not-so-subtle message from my friends, reminding me that they knew I was back on Shoppal. What has been surprising, though, is the lack of any notes or phone calls in the last few days. It gives me a creepy feeling, wondering what they'll try next."

CHAPTER NINETEEN

After taking Jester home and getting him settled on the sun porch, Damien took Trish to the one nice restaurant on the island for lunch.

"This is a pleasant surprise," she told him as he held her chair. "But are you sure you told Gordy? She will be impossible if she's fixed lunch and we don't show up."

"Good." Damien gave her a lopsided grin. "Maybe she'll quit. I can appreciate the fact that she takes her responsibilities seriously, but I'll be damned if I'll let her order me around as if I'm a two-year-old. But just to pacify the old harridan, I did call her."

"Thanks. I think that's the main reason my father let her go. He didn't like having his life run by the clock, either." Trish placed her napkin in her lap, then looked at the menu. "Oh, dear," she murmured, "I can't make up my mind."

"Let me guess," Damien said, chuckling.

"You're torn between the oysters and the shrimp. Right?"

"Don't be cute." She tried to frown. "I take my eating very seriously. Having to choose between so many delicious dishes has always been difficult."

"I know. When we were married, it got to the point where I seriously considered ordering for you rather than watching you go through the pain of not being able to eat everything on the menu."

"That is unkind." She looked down her small, straight nose at him. "You make me sound like a pig."

"You are about some things," he teased.

The waitress appeared at that moment to take their order, and Trish was forced to come to a decision. Once they were alone again, Damien looked intently at her. "Marry me, Trish. And this time I'm asking on my own, not because Hal suggested it."

He said it so quietly that she was almost positive she'd misunderstood him, but one look into his eyes told her she hadn't been mistaken. Nor was she mistaken by the sense of self-assuredness radiating from him to her. This time she knew without any doubt that he meant it. He loved her.

"You'd be taking an awful risk," she finally spoke. "Doesn't what I told you last night make you afraid?" Could she overcome her fear and give him the baby he so desperately wanted? And, if not, would she again turn into an embittered woman lashing out at the man she loved till she made their lives a living hell?

"I don't think so," he said, brushing away her cautious advice. "The only thing I would ask you to do is see a doctor. Talk with him . . . or her, whichever the case may be. But put your fears out in the open and stop being ashamed of them. You might even want to see a therapist. If you do then I'll go with you. We'll fight it together, honey."

She shook her head. It wasn't that she was so surprised by the proposal, she told herself. She knew how Damien felt about her. And even after her confession the evening before, he'd made love to her with a tenderness that left her glowing with contentment. But for once she was considering his needs, his wants. And he did want children, of that she was positive.

"What if it doesn't work out?" she asked in a pleading voice. "What then?"

"Do you love me, Trish?"

"You know I do," she was quick to reply. "Do you doubt my love?"

"No, but I wanted you to say it. Keep repeating it over and over to yourself. Deep love between two people can go a long way toward solving some very complicated problems." He reached out and caught her hand as she was toying with her knife. "I don't want you to feel as though you're deceiving me again, honey. You aren't. You've been as honest with me as you can possibly be. Put your mind on hold and do what your heart tells you."

"Do you follow that same advice?" She smiled.

"Only when it concerns you."

"Do I have to give you an answer right now?"

"Can you?" he quietly asked.

"I'm not sure," she said frankly. "I want to, but—I'm so afraid of flubbing up again."

"Well, at least that's an improvement over the last time I asked you, isn't it?" He raised her fingers to his lips, his blue eyes bold and confident. "You won't flub up, I won't let you. But I think you should know something."

"What is it?"

"I'm not leaving this island without you. So unless you want to be responsible for a wild, ragin' Texan plastering this narrow strip of land with huge billboards reading, Marry me, Trish, and scaring your neighbors half to death with my awful manners, you'll give me the answer I want."

"You really wouldn't do that, would you?" She asked the question in a joking manner, but the gleam in his eyes told her that he would, and that he'd do any number of other embarrassing things as well.

"Try me," he challenged.

"No," she said hurriedly. "I promise I'll give you an answer in two days. Okay?"

"You're a pushover in the face of a little blackmail." He released her hand and then leaned back in his chair, enormously pleased with himself.

Trish was so befuddled by the time the food arrived that she barely tasted anything. She felt like the last chicken in civilization with the remaining fox readying her for his final meal.

During the few minutes it took for them to drive home, she found herself becoming nervous and unsure of herself. Don't be a goose, she silently scolded herself. You were married to the man for three years before, and you've been sharing his bed for the last two weeks. What is there to be so uptight about?

But she knew it went deeper than the mere fact that they'd lived and made love together and knew each other's body as well as they knew their own. This time she was feeling the pressure of her own determination. A determination that left no room for failure.

Damien brought the car to a stop in the driveway, a muttered "Damn!" causing Trish to jerk out of her reverie and stare at him. She followed his narrowed gaze, then laughed.

Gordy was attacking the floor of the sun porch with the broom as if it were her mortal enemy.

"Well?" He gave Trish a resigned look. "Are you ready for our daily lecture regarding the cleanliness of the sun porch and the outbuildings as well?"

"No, but I doubt that will deter Gordy."

And it didn't. No sooner did they reluctantly get out of the car than she began. "I simply can't put up with this, Trish." She stopped long enough to push her glasses up onto the bridge of her nose and pat the tight coil of gray hair at her nape, then continued. "For the life of me I can't figure out why you insist on keeping these dogs inside when you've got a perfectly good kennel with nothing in it."

"Since it's her house and her kennel and her dogs, don't you think it should also be her decision to keep them where it suits her?" Damien asked a bit too sharply.

"Perhaps it would be better if I quit," Gordy stated, ignoring Damien and glaring at Trish. "I don't care for animals being kept in the house." She gestured toward the floor around the crates and the small amount of powder she'd swept up. "Next thing I know you'll probably have the dogs in the living room."

"I like having the dogs inside, Gordy," Trish

began, hoping to reason with the angry woman. "As for the powder, the only thing I can think of is that Dad used those same crates for some of his terriers. I'm sure there is a residue of powder in all the cracks and seams. I guess it works loose when the dogs move around."

"So you won't move the dogs to the kennel?" Gordy demanded archly.

"No," Trish answered adamantly.

Gordy leaned the broom against the wall and began removing the apron she was wearing. "You have my address," she said stubbornly. "You can mail my money to me." Without another word she walked into the kitchen, picked up her purse, then stalked past Trish and Damien and out the door.

"I hope you like cooking," Trish muttered crossly as she watched the housekeeper stalk away. "If you had been less abrupt with her she might have stayed."

When there was no reply from him, she turned and did a double take. He was down on his haunches beside the white powder Gordy had been ranting about. She was further puzzled when he caught a small amount of the white stuff between his thumb and forefinger and raised it to his nose.

Nate, who chose that moment to enter the porch from the kitchen, leaned one arm against the doorframe and regarded his brother as though trying to decide which asylum he would commit him to.

"Into a new hobby, big brother?" he asked pointedly.

Suddenly there was the strangest expression on Damien's face as he looked up at Nate. "Would you believe that Mrs. Gordon has been sweeping out no telling how much of this stuff every day?"

"Of course she has." Nate looked disgusted. "She'll sweep anything out that isn't nailed down. Damien, are you all right?"

Damien motioned for him to kneel down beside him. Nate looked at Trish, his brows raised. "Okay," he remarked facetiously as he did as instructed. "Now what?"

"Sniff. Taste."

"Sn—" Nate started to repeat, then the same remarkable change that Damien had undergone swept over him. He sniffed, a muffled exclamation erupting from his startled lips.

Trish felt the hair on her neck stand on end as she watched and listened to the amazing conversation. Was it possible? She took a hesitant step forward. "Damien? Is that what I think it is?"

"Cocaine, honey." He swiveled around and looked up at her. "No wonder poor Jester was zonked out. He had his own private stash.

Find us some hammers and screwdrivers, Trish. I think we're about to crack the case."

Hal stood staring at the neatly stacked bags of white powder that lined the bottom of each crate, a soft whistling sound coming from between his teeth. "No wonder they were after you, Trish. Do you realize how valuable this is to them?"

"Not until you told me in Florida," a dazed Trish replied. She was still trembling, still dumbfounded to discover what had been in her possession for over three months. "My God!" she said, turning pale. "What would have happened if I'd wrecked my van? There's no way on earth I could have defended myself or my father if I'd been caught with this much cocaine."

"Don't think about it now, honey." Damien hugged her to him. "I hope the worst is over."

"Not so fast, Damien. We're the only ones who know about this. We still have to wait for some move from the contact here on Shoppal," Hal told him.

"But what if they've given up?" Trish cried.

"They haven't, believe me. They've simply been thrown off stride by you having a live-in houseguest. I've got a gut feeling that all hell's about to break loose."

"I've heard that before." Trish tried not to sound disappointed.

"So my timing isn't what it should be," Hal said, giving her a cheeky grin. "There's only been one incident in days, and that involved your dog. They've got to move soon; they have too much money involved to sit back and wait."

After hashing and rehashing the probable manner in which the next move by the smugglers would come, Trish managed to get everyone into the large kitchen and seated at the long table. She made coffee and served it, then sat down next to Damien and listened.

"I still can't figure out how they could have missed that damn stuff," Hal kept repeating. He looked across at Trish. "Didn't your father use those crates for his trip to Mexico?"

"Yes," she answered him for the umpteenth time. "He carried three terriers in them."

"It doesn't make sense," he stubbornly maintained. "If those crates have been sitting on that sun porch all this time, then we have to assume we're dealing with rank amateurs."

"Oh, but they haven't—" Trish closed her eyes, her hands gripping the edge of the table in frustration. How could she have been so stupid?

"What's wrong, honey?" Damien turned and grabbed her by the arm. "Are you ill, Trish?" he asked, his face a study of concern.

"No"—she shook her head—"I'm not ill." She looked straight at Hal. "The reason those crates were never searched is because they were in Savannah at a friend's kennel. I'm so sorry."

"Tell me more, green eyes, and forget the apology," a beaming Hal urged her.

"There were two other handlers traveling with my father. When the accident occurred, they divided the dogs and the equipment he was carrying between them and brought them to Shoppal, except for five dogs that had to be shipped back to their owners."

She took a sip of coffee to ease the stiffness in her throat, then went on. "Craig Wilson kept those dogs, and the crates they were in, overnight at his kennel in Savannah. The next day he took them to the airport in airline crates and shipped them home. Our five crates, including the ones I've been using, had been sitting in his kennel until two weeks ago when I went and got them for the trip to Florida."

"And the other two crates?" Damien prompted her.

She gave him a frightened look. "They're still in Craig's kennel."

"Don't worry about your friend, Trish," Hal was quick to comfort her. "They have no way of knowing about the other crates." He leaned back in his chair, his arms crossed over his chest and a huge smile on his face. "Isn't it wonderful when you keep hammering away at something till it all falls into place?"

"Oh, it's just peachy," Damien remarked in such a scathing voice that they all laughed.

"I'll make you a bet that within twenty-four hours we'll have this case closed," Hal challenged him.

"You're on," Damien accepted. "And I've never wanted to lose a bet more."

All during the afternoon Trish felt as though she were walking on eggshells. Each time the phone would ring she would rush to answer, disappointment flooding over her when she heard the familiar voice of a friend. Do something! she cried out in her mind over and over again. But the waiting continued, and her nerves were near the breaking point. Each step of the investigation had been painful and difficult, from encountering Damien in Florida to finding the cocaine on her sun porch. It was as though she'd been fighting an enormous battle for months now, and she was worn out, physically and emotionally.

She lifted the final dish from the dishwasher and set it in the cupboard, then closed the door. After a quick glance around the kitchen to see that she'd forgotten nothing, she turned off the light and walked into the hall, intending to join Damien and Nate in the den.

She heard the sound of someone talking coming from her bedroom. She stopped and listened. For a moment there was silence, then Trish caught the sound of Damien's voice. He was obviously talking on the phone. Once again she started to walk away, but the sound of her own name halted her. Silently she walked along the carpeted hall to the edge of the door.

"It's no laughing matter," Damien snapped. "If she ever finds out that I came to Florida because we suspected her of smuggling cocaine, I will personally rearrange your grinning face."

For long moments Trish stood immobile, too shocked to move. Damien had lied to her from the very first. Suddenly she wanted to lash out at him, wanted to do him bodily harm. She took two steps into the room, then halted.

He was a miserable, low-down bastard! Lies had spewed from his lips for two weeks. Lies that she had believed, lies that had her condemning herself for not being truthful with him. God! she quietly raged, she must be the biggest sap in the world.

"If you're so cocksure of yourself, why don't you try to explain?" she heard Damien growl. He slammed down the receiver, then got to his feet. Suddenly he froze. Like a man sleepwalking, he slowly turned and faced a grim-faced Trish standing in the doorway.

For several long, gut-wrenching moments he stared at her, committing to memory each and every angry feature of her face. "You heard?" His voice sounded harsh and bitter.

"Enough to know that you're a double-dealing bastard," she flung at him. "I want you out of my house this instant." Her temples were pounding, and a cold film of perspiration had broken out over her body.

"Please listen to me, Trish," he pleaded for the first time in his life with a woman. But this wasn't just any woman, he told himself. This was Trish. This was his life he was begging for.

Without forethought or plan her hand dropped to the desk just to her right. Her fingers closed around a heavy crystal dish. With only one thought in mind she raised her arm and hurled the dish at his head. With the sound of breaking glass shattering the silence, she turned on her heel and ran from the room.

Before she could reach the door of the kitchen, she heard Damien yell out her name, then the sound of his heavier tread as he bounded after her. In front of her she saw an astonished Nate appear in the doorway, his mouth agape as he watched. It was his sudden, looming presence that caused Trish to make the mistake of coming to a momentary halt.

The next thing she was aware of was a band of steel around her waist and an iron grip clasping her shoulder. "Trish," Damien rasped in her ear, his breath coming out in brutal gasps, "you are going to listen to me if I have to hog-tie you."

"Take your lying hands off me. You're despicable." Trish twisted and squirmed, her face a picture of outrage. In the middle of her struggles she threw a nasty look at Nate. "Help me, you gutless wimp."

"Stay out of this, Nate," Damien said, grunting, a burst of air rushing from his mouth as one of Trish's elbows banged against his ribs. "Damn it, Trish, calm down before you hurt yourself," he yelled in her ear.

"Go to hell, you lying jackass."

"I did not lie to you," he ranted manically.

For a moment Trish forgot to struggle. Her head swung around, and she stared disbelievingly at him. "You're incredible! I heard you with my own ears. I heard you discussing how to keep your little secret of why you 'accidentally' appeared in Florida. Were you hoping I'd get a life sentence in some prison?" she yelled.

"You heard parts of a one-sided conversation," he ground out from between clenched teeth.

"I heard enough." She whammed down her heel on the toe of his shoe.

"Ouch!" Damien shouted. "Damn you, that hurt."

"I sincerely hope so. Now maybe you can understand a little of how I feel," she hissed at him, showing no mercy.

"Er . . . may I interrupt for one tiny moment?" Nate asked.

Both struggling parties came to a halt, their flushed faces glaring at him with mulish contempt. "Butt out!" Damien snapped.

"I would simply like to point out to Trish that the story Hal told you when he came to Texas was overwhelmingly against her. I'd also like her to know that nothing mattered to you but the hope of proving her innocent. I remember the first thing that you told me when I arrived at the motel was that you knew she was innocent." He let his gaze slip to a less combative Trish. "That man holding you worships you. And even if you had been the grande dame of the cocaine racket, he would have stood by you. I'd think twice, if I were you, before I threw away a love as deep and strong as his." He turned on his heel and walked back down the hall and closed the door.

Their first moment alone was awkward. Damien cleared his throat nervously and dropped his hands to his sides. Trish ducked her head, her gaze glued to her fingers as they pulled at a loose string hanging from the hem of the overblouse she was wearing. She felt like a first-class idiot, and she hadn't the remotest idea how to make amends.

"If you keep pulling at that you're going to unravel the hem," Damien said quietly beside her. His hand followed his voice and caught her chin in his gentle grasp. He forced her head up so that he could see her face.

"I want you to know here and now that I would have done or will do anything in my power to protect you. And if I could have gotten you back by never revealing the fact that at one time Hal suspected you, I would have done so. I have a set of morals by which I've always tried to live, Trish, but where you're concerned, I have nothing but a love for you that knows no bounds."

Trish felt tears stinging her eyes. Slowly they began to slip over the edges and trail down her cheeks. She stepped closer to him, so close that the tips of her breasts were pressing against his chest. "Please forgive me for not trusting you," she said in a trembling voice. "I couldn't stand the thought of you believing that I would do such a thing as becoming involved in drugs. I guess I went a little crazy."

"Oh, no"—Damien smiled down at her, his hands closing over her buttocks and bringing all of her against him—"not a little crazy, my darling witch; you went wild. If I hadn't dodged that damn bowl you threw at me, I'd probably have a six-inch gash in my head by now. And I'm positive that one of my toes is broken." He dipped his head and kissed her until she was struggling for air. He raised his head, his eyes dulled with passion. "Marry me, Trish."

"I will, my darling, I will. And I pray with all my heart that I can give you a son."

His face contorted, and his arms, holding her, trembled as a deep shudder rippled throughout his body. "Only when you're ready sweetheart, only when you're ready." He swung her into his arms, his gaze never leaving her face as he made his way to the bedroom and slammed the door with his foot.

CHAPTER TWENTY

The next morning began with an early visit from Hal. He not only confirmed Damien's suspicions regarding Wyatt Jamison, but he also informed an astonished Trish that Wyatt was a prime suspect in a smuggling operation that not only included drugs but art as well.

A sense of sadness stayed with her as she dressed for work, then sat quietly beside Damien as he drove her over to the shop.

"I know I've made some unkind remarks about Jamison," he awkwardly remarked, "and I still don't like him. But you do, and I'm sorry he's disappointed you."

"Thank you," she said, managing a tiny smile, but her heart wasn't in it. "I suppose I've learned more about human failings and triumphs in the last four months than most people learn in a lifetime."

"There's only one thing you haven't learned," he said seriously.

"What's that?"

"How to be a meek, submissive wife."

The remark elicited the smile he wanted to see, and Trish felt better. It was amazing, she thought as they got out of the car and entered the shop. When she was upset, he consoled her. When she was alone and in danger, he stormed the enemy and tried to rescue her. She wasn't sure she was deserving of that kind of love.

In midmorning Damien got a call from Hal, wanting him to rush right over. Nate was called to the shop and immediately got into an argument with Millie.

While they took good-natured swipes at one another in the front room, Trish busied herself with the monthly statements. She was halfway through when she discovered that she'd taken two files home with her the evening before and had promptly forgotten them.

Without thinking she pushed back her chair and reached for her purse. She walked into the front room and told Millie the problem. "You don't have to go with me, Nate. I'll only be gone a few minutes."

"Not on your life, kiddo," he said, switching from an incredible tease to a stern watchdog. "I remember you going to the ladies' room once and returning to your motel by way of the emergency room."

"Say no more." She shuddered.

As she sat beside Nate in the car Trish was so busy remembering the evening she'd spent in Damien's arms that she failed to notice the dark frown that had come over his face. It took his muttered "Damn fool" and the sound of a speeding car passing them unnecessarily close to bring her back to the present. They were traveling on the beach road, which some of the teenagers considered a perfect speedway.

"Probably some of the summer kids showing off to their friends," Trish offered. "From the way some of them drive I'm surprised we don't have more accidents."

"I agree." At that moment another car came zooming up behind them. Nate eased the Continental over as far as possible, hoping to avoid another near accident.

But instead of passing as the other car had done, the driver drew alongside and began to edge them off the blacktop. "Those aren't college kids, Trish," Nate spoke hurriedly. "I think your fan club has decided to talk to you personally."

"Oh, my God, Nate!" she cried as she tried to brace herself for the collision she knew was coming. "What on earth can we do?"

"Just try to stay ca— whoops, I spoke too soon." He nodded grimly. "I do believe their friends are coming back to help."

Trish looked up to see the first car bearing down on them.

Suddenly there was no place left to go but down the concrete seawall or straight into the car coming toward them.

The next few minutes were a total confusion in Trish's mind. She had a hazy sensation of seeing Nate turn the car toward the bay. The next thing she knew, he was fumbling with her seat belt, then pushing her unceremoniously from the car, his agile body close behind.

As soon as they hit the ground Nate caught her wrist in a steel grip and pulled her after him. "Kick off those damn high heels, Trish, and run for all you're worth," he shouted at her.

As she sprinted for her life the crazy thought rushed through her mind that someday she would probably have a good laugh over the spectacle they must have made as they raced along, but at that moment, all she was capable of concentrating on was trying to keep up with Nate.

They'd gone several yards when there was a peculiar popping noise behind them, closely followed by a chorus of raised voices. A small cabin cruiser that had been anchored offshore began coming inland. Sirens could be heard, their shrill call drawing nearer and nearer.

Nate chanced a quick look over his shoulder and then came to a halt. He transferred his hold from Trish's wrist to her shoulder and pressed her down to the sand. "We . . . can . . . stop, Trish," he gasped, taking huge, gulping breaths of air into his lungs. "Look." He pointed back up the beach to where they'd begun their frantic flight. "They've caught them." Without another word he dropped to his knees, then flopped back on the sand.

Trish, her own labored breathing making it impossible to speak, watched as cars bearing state troopers arrived on the scene. Two men from the cabin cruiser were involved in a wrestling match with the occupants of one of the vehicles, while others could be seen being led to the trooper's cars.

Her head drooped forward, and an overwhelming sense of relief swept over her as she realized the nightmare was finally coming to an end. The sound of running feet behind her caused her to look around.

"Trish? Are you all right?" Damien asked, dropping to his knees beside her and taking her in his arms.

"Is it over?" She drew back so that she could see his face.

"It's over. Hal and the other agents are thrilled as kids at a birthday party. But I'm afraid your friend Wyatt is in for a difficult time, honey. He's been the brains behind the operation here on Shoppal for a number of years. One of Decker's deputies was only too happy to tell everything he knew in order to plea-bargain. Decker and Jamison should be in custody by now."

"Have they learned who murdered my father?"

He looked at her for several seconds, then pulled her hard against his chest, his arms tight around her. "It was Decker. He was searching for the cocaine. John was supposed to be away for a couple of hours. He got back earlier than expected and found Decker in the kennel."

"Somehow that doesn't surprise me."

"Are you sure you're all right?" he questioned her. "You seem to be taking all this very calmly."

Trish smiled. "Whatever hysteria I possessed was used up ages ago. As for being calm, if you had a two-hundred-pound-plus man bounce you out of a car and force you to run down a beach at breakneck speed, you'd also be calm. I'm not able to be anything else."

"How's that for gratitude?" Nate broke in. "I risk life and limb to keep her safe, and she complains." He sat up, then looked back at the distance they'd run. "If I never see another stretch of sandy white beach again, I'll be just as happy."

Damien reached around Trish and clasped his brother on the shoulder. "Thanks, Nate." No other words were spoken. The look that passed between them was enough.

Nate had taken Millie to dinner. Trish smiled to herself as she saw the fate of her brother-in-law becoming clearer by the second. Hal was lying down in one of the guest bedrooms, trying to catch up on some of the sleep he'd missed over the past few weeks. He had a lengthy vacation coming and had threatened anyone who disturbed him.

The case had been gone over from at least a dozen different angles. Trish had made endless pots of coffee and listened to countless thoughts on why this or that had happened. Thankfully, she thought, sighing, it always came out with the same ending. The culprits had been caught.

There was only one question that remained unanswered in her mind as she and Damien took a late walk along the beach. "How did you and Hal get to us so quickly?"

"Simple, really. I was with him when the call came in from the agents watching the shop, telling him that you and Nate were leaving. They followed you. When they caught sight of the two cars and the erratic behavior of the drivers, they radioed for help and moved in."

"So it really wasn't necessary for us to streak out across the sand, was it?"

"Indeed it was. Hal was convinced they were going to kidnap you, and Nate, since he was with you. Wyatt's little visit to the house the other day wasn't nearly as innocent as it appeared to be. He finally admitted to that under questioning. Can you imagine what must have been running through his mind when he saw the 'powder' and watched Gordy sweeping it out? Thousands of dollars a day being swept away."

Their laughter was refreshing and without restraint. When the sound of it faded away, Trish's face became somber. "I really do have a lot to be grateful to Nate for, don't I?"

"So do I, honey, so do I." He brought their walk to a halt by slipping his arms around her. "I love you."

"And I love you."

"Will you marry me as soon as I can arrange it?"

"I'll marry you today if you can arrange it." And in her heart she knew she would give him children, for Damien had accepted her without any stipulations. The only demand he was placing on her was that she love him, a demand she eagerly accepted.

"Then I think you should do some quick packing for a trip west." He smiled down at her. "I can't take any chances on you changing your mind."

"Don't worry," Trish said, grinning at him. "This time you've got me for good."